"I take exception to the characterization of my hair as 'difficult,' as my hair is in fact perfect, which I can prove in a court of law. Everything else James wrote is exactly as it happened, to the best of my memory."
—JUNO TEMPLE, *prodigiously talented actress with perfect hair*

"James Greer has always been a novelist I would hock my skills set to measure up against, but even matched against his prior coups, *Bad Eminence* is unspeakably exciting. Its grace and hilarity and brains and foolproof read on Frenchness and I don't even know what else made my hands shake."   —DENNIS COOPER

"With eye and ear and tongue—and oh brother, what a tongue!—James Greer is the leading Renaissance Man for our current and possibly terminal Dark Ages."   —JOSHUA COHEN

"*Bad Eminence* is, at one and the same time, a diatribe against narrative; a fiendishly engaging mystery; a learned disputation on the arts of translation; a masterful addition to the literature of sisters and twins; a roman à clef (I'll never tell); a catalogue raisonné of the French nouveau roman; and the most literate advert for Bolivian firewater you'll ever encounter. By turns wildly maddening, laugh-out-loud funny, heartrendingly poignant, *Bad Eminence* pulls you into its world like no other. You will not regret a moment spent romping in its lexical playfields."   —HOWARD A. RODMAN

"This is a work of lacerating style that shook my faith in the tangible world. It preys upon the real in capricious ways, like so much of the best fiction, toying with the reader's memories until we're not sure what we see, or what we have seen. James Greer is a circus-master of great humor, malevolence, and allusion, a fabricator of eerie truths. It's terrifying to enter his world." —MICHAEL LESSLIE

"The narrator of James Greer's *Bad Eminence*, Vanessa Salomon, comes on like a double-deranged cross of Tristram Shandy and Charles Kinbote only twice as funny and half as self-aware. What makes it work is Greer's pinpoint control of Vanessa's ineffably charming voice (and, uh, her incredible cocktail recipes! Pour yourself a Vieux Carré, why don't you?), and his diabolical ability to make her digressions amount to something. (Also, did I mention the cocktail recipes?) If this book has flaws, I didn't notice them. *Bad Eminence* is a stone blast from start to finish." —MATTHEW SPECKTOR

"James Greer is the Daphne de Maurier of psychological French literary translation thrillers that don't in any legally actionable way involve Michel Houellebecq. *Bad Eminence* is a funny, witty walk into a world where words, memories, people, life, death, and truth have more than one meaning." —BEN SCHWARTZ

PRAISE FOR JAMES GREER

"James Greer's *The Failure* is such an unqualified success, both in conception and execution, that I have grave doubts he actually wrote it." —STEVEN SODERBERGH

"*Artificial Light* skates on the purity of confession. It's a brutal reveal; an Abyss Narrative with hooks. Read it in a rush of abomination and rise above, rise above." —STEPHEN MALKMUS

BAD
EMINENCE

Bad
Eminence

JAMES GREER

SHEFFIELD – LONDON – NEW YORK

First published in 2022 by
And Other Stories
Sheffield – London – New York
www.andotherstories.org

1 3 5 7 9 8 6 4 2

ISBN: 9781913505349
eBook ISBN: 9781913505356

Editor: Jeremy M. Davies; Copy-editor: Robina Pelham Burn; Proofreader:
Sarah Terry; Typeset in Albertan Pro and Linotype Syntax by Tetragon,
London; Cover Design: Tom Etherington; Photography: Edward Kucherenko
(portrait) and Erik van Dijk (swan); Printed and bound on acid-free,
age-resistant Munken Premium by CPI Limited, Croydon, UK.

And Other Stories gratefully acknowledge that our work is
supported using public funding by Arts Council England.

to Lola

CONTENTS

This is a true story. Everything in this book happened exactly in the manner depicted herein, and all the characters are unembellished portrayals of actual living and/or dead persons. No names have been changed, no liberties taken. All dialogue has been transcribed verbatim. And fuck you if you think any of this [expansive arm gesture] is funny. It's not funny.

Should you have any difficulty in untangling any of the following, the management recommends you check in with the Help Desk.

Somewhere, deep inside you, hidden by all sorts of fears and worries and petty little thoughts, is a clean pure being made of radiant colors.

SHIRLEY JACKSON
Hangsaman

On the eleventh of December 1942, a child was born to the Breunn family of Bury St Edmunds, Suffolk, England. His name was T. Edward Breunn – and that's all we know. As most authors and publishers would prefer of their translators, Mr Breunn managed to make himself so invisible as to have left nearly no evidence of his passage through this world. What little has been recorded is due only to the diligence of some librarian back in the age of paper. He or she made note of the above details, and no others, on the original, analogue, card-catalogue entries for his little-known English version of Kafka's *The Trial* (1981). Later, presumably, these entries were transcribed with neither comment nor correction and entered into the great digital record in the sky.

I can find no record of his death. We'll just have to assume the best.

But, the thing is, I'm working on my own translation of Robbe-Grillet's *Souvenirs du triangle d'or*, and Breunn is responsible for the only extant edition in English. And Breunn's isn't bad, credit where it's due, but I'm not so sure he could actually speak French. I think I can do better. I was born in a trilingual household, you see – French, English and money – so I'm as comfortable in each as in my own skin.

Which is to say, *mostly.* Better, being able to speak money fluently means there aren't many other languages that won't yield to you with just a whisper in the tongue of tongues. I'm also conversant with Latin, Russian, German, Italian, Spanish, Portuguese, Romanian, Swedish, Norwegian, Finnish, Icelandic . . . Take my word for it.

How, you may ask, can I say that Breunn's *Souvenirs* isn't bad when he didn't know the language? Well, funny story. There are a fuckton of competing theories out there about translating, from Walter Benjamin to Hilaire Belloc to Paul Ricoeur to Susan Sontag to Hannah Arendt to R. Pevear to A.S. Wohl to L. Davis to J. Malcolm to every person who's ever read a book. But let me sum up: nobody can agree what makes a good translation; nobody can agree what makes a bad translation; everybody agrees that it would be ideal if everyone could read the original work in the original language; everybody knows this is impossible.

Beyond or alongside these widely acknowledged (by translators) competitive dogmas, the history of translation is fraught with eccentrics, frauds and prodigiously talented amateurs, without which much of the world's literature would remain inaccessible to most of the world's readers. Lin Shu couldn't read a word of any foreign language, but in the early twentieth century translated something like two hundred works of Western literature – Shakespeare, Tolstoy, Dickens and so on – into classical Chinese, on the basis of a plot paraphrase from a polyglot friend. Simon Leys claimed that Lin Shu somehow managed, through a superior command of style in his native tongue, to improve in many cases on the originals. He's an outlier, I think we can agree. Also that's not translation so much as, you know, writing.

The Torah's third-century BCE translation into Greek famously took seventy (or seventy-two, depending on who's counting, though even this has been challenged, notably in 1684 by Humphry Hody, a name I did not make up) Alexandria-based scholars to render from the original Hebrew, despite which or possibly because of which they still got a lot of stuff wrong, with repercussions that reverberate still among the religiously disposed. The Vulgate or Latin translation of the Bible, produced mostly by St Jerome in the late fourth century CE and later revised in 1592 by a troupe of performing angels, introduced — right at the top, I might add — a mistake that has slandered the entirely innocent apple (is any fruit entirely innocent, though?) down through the centuries. It was a fig, people. If you don't believe me, consult Northrop Frye's *The Great Code*. And don't even get me started on the King James Version, another translation by committee that proves . . . I don't know what it proves, exactly. Because for every grievous error perpetrated by that Jacobean assemblage, any number of foundational turns of phrase — without which cliché-mongers would be bereft of such succulents as 'a drop in the bucket', 'a fly in the ointment' and 'a labour of love' — would have gone missing forever from the collective minds of anglophone civilisation.

Sometimes a really outstanding author whose book might otherwise be considered untranslatable (though, as noted above, there's a sense in which all books are untranslatable) is fluent in several languages and can oversee a given translation themselves, as was the case in, e.g. *Ulysses'* French rendering, though 'oversee' is maybe an unfortunately ableist term considering Joyce was mostly blind at that point. But that's as rare as Joyce himself was rare. His interest in all languages or in surpassing language itself (using language), particularly in *Finnegans Wake*, while possibly a doomed undertaking, incorporates translation into the writing, which is sort of the opposite of what Lin Shu did.

On the antipodal pole, may I present Constance Garnett, whose Englished versions of Russian classics you likely grew up reading, assuming you read Russian classics growing up, and which are objectively terrible as translations but are responsible in large part for popularising those authors (Tolstoy and Dostoevsky in particular) with the English-speaking public. So while it's true that if you read her version of *Anna Karenina* you are reading Constance Garnett as much as – if not more than – you are reading Tolstoy, at least you are palpating Tolstoy's bones, and there now exist much better, or at least more accurate, translations of his work for your edification, or whatever you read books for.

Xavier Hadley, a much lesser-known light than Ms Garnett, possibly because he chose only to translate into Scottish Gaelic (his best known work is *Foirm na n-Urrnuidheadh*, a version of John Knox's *Book of Common Order*), had the curious habit of sketching his first drafts on dried peas with a tiny brush made from the plucked hairs of a common housefly, without the use of a microscope. It will perhaps tell you something about the special nature of the community of professional translators (we have our own magazine!) that Hadley is considered by some a bit of a show-off, but on the whole sound in his approach.

It reduces over low heat to this: you try to get down as best you can what the writer has written while also reproducing the way the writer wrote it — but in another language. With all its different rhythms, idioms, vocabularies. You try to make the reader reading in the target language believe they're reading what the original writer wrote, had the original writer written in the reader's language: a magic trick seldom executed with apodictic success. Howlers are as ineluctable as the modality of the visible; but one can on occasion by careful and patient application of the intellect, if that's the word I want, find elegant solutions to problems of inelegance. That's the shit I live for.

There's no money in it, so it's good I don't need money. The crucial aspect, from my tendentious POV, is that you love the writer you're translating. The ones I love are precisely the ones who call themselves, or get themselves called, *untranslatable*. The stylists, the weirdos, the outsiders and innovators. Which makes and has made them extremely difficult. But when it's an *ardorous* task, it's never *arduous*. Hold your applause, please.

If I've done my job right, I will have made myself vanish as entirely as Mr Breunn's *prénom*. The writer is, and ought to be, the star of the show. The translator ought to be, in the best sense of the word, invisible. Does that bother me, you ask? Let's say it doesn't bother me anymore. It may even be that I've come to enjoy that part of the job most.

Shit. There's the doorbell. Hold on while I . . . oh, it's my upstairs neighbour. She's never home. I suppose I'll have to — socialise.

2

Juno. It is Juno, right? Juno Temple? I think I saw you in a movie by . . . I can't remember who by. A well-known director. You were fantastic. I'm sure you're always fantastic.

Anyway. Please come in. Call me Van. Short for Vanessa. Or just V. Make yourself at home. My etc. is your etc. That's a Tracey Emin. Next to it is a Sophie Taeuber-Arp. Astonishing, no?

I draw your attention to the series of Francesca Woodman prints on the other wall. I'm obsessed with her. One of the reasons I bought this apartment – but I expect you're thirsty.

Might I suggest a round of Singani Sours? They're quite *séduisant*, and, you know, small translation presses can use all the product-placement cash they can wrangle, in this fallen world of ours.

2 OZ SINGANI 63
.75 OZ LEMON JUICE
.75 OZ AGAVE
1 EGG WHITE
2 DASHES ANGOSTURA BITTERS

DRY SHAKE FIRST FOUR INGREDIENTS,
THEN SHAKE AGAIN WITH ICE. STRAIN
INTO A GLASS AND TOP WITH BITTERS.

SOUR

Please, sit. I'll bring your drink. Frank Gehry designed that sofa. And the two chairs. They're not especially comfortable, but I adore that shade of violet.

À *propos de bottes*, are you hungry? I've got some snack-type items that would go well with the drinks. The book you're looking at is a novel by Alain Robbe-Grillet, noted writer, film-maker and pervert. It's an English translation of his *Souvenirs du triangle d'or*. The title's been rendered as *Recollections of the Golden Triangle*, which is solid. It's a solid translation. You're welcome to borrow it. The novel – we'll get to that soon. A fair representative of the so-called school of the *nouveau roman*, in its decadent phase. Not that I'm much for schools of literature. Wouldn't we all rather be taken on our own terms, as individuals? If any of us qualify as individuals. I probably qualify even less than you.

That said, I admire many of the *nouveau roman* writers. Nathalie Sarraute, Marguerite Duras, Maurice Blanchot, Robert Pinget, Claude Simon: all wonderful. Some of the radical textual experiments that followed – Georges Perec's lipogrammatic *La disparition*, for example, where he writes without using the letter 'e' – to say nothing of the more outré Oulipo efforts – are less interesting to me. *La disparition* would have been amusing to translate, though. Gilbert Adair got there before me. (And Ian Monk before him, though his version has been sitting in a drawer for going on fifty years now. What, did you think translators don't suffer the same heartbreak as authors, sometimes, drinking themselves to sleep over the work the world may never see?)

In my defence, I was two years old when the Adair version was published, so could hardly toss my hat into the ring. A

Void is Adair's title in English. It's not as good as the original, but what is?

Are you in a hurry or anything? The reason I ask, you're in a posish to do me a huge favour, should you be so reclined – that's a joke because you picked the couch, that is to say, the *recliner*. Which was the smart choice! Most comfortable piece of furniture in my under-furnished place. Gosh, I don't know why I'm so nervous all of a sudden.

You're an actress, right? I mean, you *act*. That's what you do, and thus what or who you are. I've just finished writing what, for lack of a better word, we'll call a book. It might even be a translation, or a kind of translation, at least in the sense that every book is a translation of the writer's experience into language, that is to say into words, which are little vehicles of sense that you can carry from one place to another like, um, dried peas. What I'd like to do is read what I've written out loud, to you. Right now. I've signed a contract with a rather unusual publisher, and before I turn in the manuscript, I'd feel better if I had some feedback from a real, live actual person, which, I have been assured by people who understand these things, you are.

Really? You would? That's so . . . kind! Assuming you actually exist and are in my loft at this moment, which is never something I take for granted, for reasons that will I hope become clear – that is just . . . very kind of you. Another Singani Sour? Paper ain't free.

How the wind doth blow! That glass is supposed to be hurricane-proof, though how it'll hold up if a car comes flying off the streets – as doesn't seem beyond possible – I can but guess. Skeins of fat rain lashing the wet streets, lashing too the traffic lights and street lamps and gingko trees. What's the word Epictetus used to describe the faculty of volition? Proairesis. That's the bugger. How will you face the end of the world? If you're a follower of Epictetus, with equanimity. If you're not, and I'm not, we'll find out when we get there. Dunno if the end of the world is nigh, exactly, but it's far from far.

I'll start reading, then.

A metaphor is a ladder to the truth but is not itself true. Think on that while I give the teacher a blowjob under his desk.

On we go. Not down but not explicitly up. Only on. A direction without direction, uncompassed, recursively discursive: a spiral in a glass globe.

Est aliquid prodisse tenus.

4

That last bit was Latin. Do you know Latin? So few people study it anymore. I mean, to be fair, there's not much interest in live languages, never mind dead ones, in the early stages of the education of most children. It's not useful, and therefore not important. Also, fyi, the blowjob was metaphorical. The teacher, the desk: metaphors.

But the ladder is real. And I'm about to pull it away. Promise me that you'll fall. That sounds dramatic, doesn't it? Like 'Ooh, scary, V. Books can't hurt anyone. Least of all the kind of books that *you* like.'

But seriously – you have to promise.

Too much throat-clearing, do you think? Too much mere exordium? Am I writing cheques that my perfect ass can't cash? It *is* perfect, by the way. Better now just to slice straight into the dark meat of the narrative. Except it's not really a narrative, per se. I hope you're not expecting a story in the trad sense. We'll come back to the beginning at the end, because that's how the spinning world works. There's a way of looking at things that suggests I spend my whole life dressing for dinner in the jungle. But that's just philosophy. Let's continue.

I am younger by two minutes than my identical twin, but I have always been the extrovert. Angelica was criminally shy throughout childhood and adolescence, a quiet, bookish girl, whereas I was the gregarious, noisy flirt daring the boys on the playground to kiss me: smacking them silly when they were too scared to try and sillier still when they weren't. My mother loved both of us, she said, but all things being equal − and they were, in this case − *me* she actually *liked*. That's how it felt, anyway. I could apply to them for a less unilateral reading of those years − my parents are alive, and together − but we rarely talk. I live in New York City, they live in Paris. Different time zones, different sensibilities, and my father's slipping into senility, which makes me all squirmy. I never know what to do with sick people. I don't have any of the feelings you're supposed to have: pity, sorrow, anger, indifference, orange soda, yellow-blue vase, black lacquer cabinet. I'm only uneasy.

I don't think they've noticed that we aren't really on speaking terms. My current stand-offishness set against my past stand-offishness wouldn't rate a complaint from my parents, especially now that I'm no longer under their purview. A different matter growing up. Growing up I was a handful.

I started smoking at twelve, drinking at thirteen, fucking at fourteen, and spent my *lycée* years talking my way into and out of trouble. At seventeen I wanted to be an actor. A famous French director was casting a part that called for a lot of nudity. I had no problem with a lot of nudity. I'm an exhibitionist. I've always liked the way my body looks. No harm in that. I should have gotten the part. I'm a good actor, and I was, modesty aside, a knockout. But I didn't get the part.

Angelique de Saxe, née Angelica Salomon, got the part. My sister accompanied me to the casting because she followed me everywhere in those days. Sure, like a little dog. Or not so little, because we were both tall, but still – a dog. A gangly dog with big tits. The director, an old lecher, liked what he saw in me, but liked more what he saw in Angelica, sitting cross-legged on the floor in the waiting area in her school uniform reading a book. A *certain virginal quality*, the paedophile called it, and after ten minutes of pretending not to want to read for the part, Angelica read for the part. You know the rest. The *succès de scandale*, the raves, the blockbuster films, the modelling contracts, the red carpet events, the awards. The glamour, the fame. Hers, and yet – but for a happenstance – mine!

Did Angelica have a certain virginal quality, after all? Of course she did. She was a virgin. I could not asseverate that designation, nor would I have wanted to, but I certainly could have acted the part, and would have, had she not followed me to the audition and stolen my life.

Here is a picture of the statue of Winged Victory in the Louvre:

6

We grew up in a labyrinthine apartment in the Île Saint-Louis in Paris. We lived in the top two floors of a three-storey Beaux Arts building on Quai de Béthune at the corner of Rue Pouelletier in the 4th arrondissement. The furniture was superannuated, fusty and leathern, and the flaking yellow paint on the walls throughout I strongly suspected had once been bright white; but what our house's interior lacked in style it made up for in books. There were books everywhere, and bookshelves built from floor to ceiling in almost every room (the kitchen being a notable exception, though the lack of shelving didn't stop us from piling books in there anyway). My dad ran the Île-de-France Film Commission, my mum was (still is, I think) a painter of some renown, a neo-neo-realist whose speciality was portraits, usually of celebrities, but from the neck down. She wouldn't paint their faces. That was the gimmick. In order to be a successful painter you have to have a gimmick. This has never not been true. Her studio took up the *rez-de-chaussée* (in fact we owned the whole building, fine), but we rarely went in there.

Her paintings sold briskly for outlandish prices; but to me, my mother's paintings might as well have been wallpaper, because that was their function in our apartment. The only one I *noticed* was a portrait of me and my sister that hung in our bedroom (we shared a bedroom until age ten; it was a large bedroom). It was unusual in that Mum had painted our faces, for reasons that she never explained. Also unexplained was the decision to hang the portrait in our shared bedroom, though there are greater mysteries in life. Can't believe I ever looked so innocent, even at eight years old. As I grew up and out of the shared bedroom, the painting advanced to a hallway I passed every day on the way to the bathroom, and through some reverse Wildean alchemy, I grew less and less like the sweet young girl in my mother's painting, and more and more like – whoever it is you're reading right now.

My body changed, and drastically, starting at about twelve years old, but those aren't the changes that registered when I compared my childhood portrait to my teenaged face in the mirror. My adolescent eyes knew something that I didn't yet know I knew. In an adult you would call it scorn, but in a teen – perhaps the foreshadow of an intuited future outlook, expressed also in the slant of my smile, and in my words any time I opened my wide mouth wide and commented, acerbically, on everything. My wit had teeth as sharp as my actual incisors, and I was fast in every sense of the word. Unlike my sister, who was as demure as I was immodest – but, may it please the court, who turned out the turncoat? I may have withered a few plump egos on the vine with my invective, but I was never volitionally dishonest. I was blunt, I was impolitic, I was rude, and much of the time obnoxious. I was a hoyden, in short. A loud, dirty, boozy girl – such are always in demand. But I told the truth. I didn't have an agenda. If you had the intelligence of a soap dish, I told you so. If your face resembled a rotting meat balloon, I told you so. Right into said face. Never behind your back, which looked like a botulistic sausage. I delivered my observations with savour and stuck round to watch the dismay work its way across your casing.

Angelica and I were outwardly alike. The same large, expressive, mallow-green eyes, the same golden-brown complexion, even — before she dyed it black at M. Kidfucker's request (and decided to keep it that way) — the same russet hair, now blonde, now red, depending on the season or the light. I'll take my jasper locks over her inky quills any day of the trip. Our lips are bee-stung and rose pink, though A has taken to wearing the brightest, glossiest shade of red lipstick available, the better to contrast with her artificially marmoreal skin and jet hair. It's an effective look, if your idea of effective is to project a frigid, unapproachable allure, but you can't argue with its success in her case.

7

Angelica's not stupid, either. Though she didn't go on to university, and I did, she was as eager a reader as I was before I went pro. We were both raging bibliophages, but I'll note that she would read any *roman de gare* lying in the remainders pile at Fnac. Me, I have standards. I was – am – a snob. Though I'd ingurgitated Agatha Christie and Inspector Maigret mysteries by the score when I was eight or nine, by the time puberty hit (and I hit back, hard) I transposed to more literary vittles. The classics, of course: everything in French and English and Russian and Latin and German (my five best languages at the time) that I could get my hands on: *La Mare au diable*; *Asinus aureus*; *Мелкий бес*; *The Expendable Man*; *Maldoror*; *I Am Your Sister*; *Peau noire, masques blancs*; *Paraphrase über den Fund eines Handschuhs*; *Malleus Maleficarum*; *Giovanni's Room*; *Le Jardin des supplices*; *Out to Lunch*; *Céline et Julie vont en bateau*; *Intercourse*; *April Galleons*; *Elemente und Ursprünge totaler Herrschaft*; *Les Fruits d'Or*; *Speedboat*; *Some Disordered Interior Geometries*; *Ceddo*; *Introduction à la littérature fantastique*; *Behind the Green Door*; *The Waves*; *Sans toit ni loi*; *Лебединый стан*; *Liber de Veritate Catholicae Fidei contra errores Infidelium*; *L'enfer* (Barbusse); *Über den Begriff der Geschichte*;

La Nébuleuse du Crabe; *Hyènes*; but what really lifts my boat off the rocks of day-to-day is language, purity-wise and simplicitudinally speaking . . . not so much a gripping story, a ripping yarn. While I would never argue that the *what* of a story is irrelevant, I would and will argue that the *way* of its telling is the *plupart* of its charm.

Not everyone would agree. After all, we're drowning-not-waving in a wide sarcastic sea of idiots. I don't mean to be judgmental. I *am* judgmental, but I don't mean to be. The gamut of my assessments and the vigour with which I convey them can be off-putting. I intend no slight to those who hold contrary opinions, nor does the phrase *wide sarcastic sea of idiots* connote anything but a damnable weakness for ludic structures and un-bons mots. I seek merely to make a pre-emptive public service announcement *in re* those disposed to drag people for habitual incivility. Please be advised: I truck not with civility, still less with habits. I had a habit of pulling at my cuticles with my teeth, until I developed a whitlow on my left index finger. Learned not to truck with habitude after that. As for civility, it's best left to courtiers, suck-ups and acolytes. Like heroin, it's more effective in widely spaced doses.

So while *story* might be a useful, even imperative convention, I am not a conventional person. Neither am I unconventional for its own sake; there are rules and regulations I observe despite wishing for better formulae. Exempli gratia: unfamiliar, untranslated words and phrases from other languages are set in italics in traditional English-language typesetting – unless, like *exempli gratia*, they happen to appear in the dictionary of record. Similarly, in common English usage, one is meant to employ those same italics when one refers in print to a published book, or indeed to a play, film, LP or long-form musical composition. Of course one can also use them for emphasis – though too much of this is frowned upon in our miserly era – which led, in my reading youth, to the impression that foreign words and movie titles are meant always to be spoken *louder* than ordinary English. And perhaps they ought to be. But for a polyglot and bibliomane at her laptop, it's a serious pain to have to go back and italicise every time I venture outside the constraints of this island English, or happen to mention a book, any book, even the book I might be writing or translating. Like Bartleby, I would prefer not to.

But I can't single-handedly rewrite the rules. I know, because I've tried. You'd think that dealing, as I tend to, with smaller publishers, who if you believe the hype are more willing to take risks, that I wouldn't have trouble finding an editor willing to turn a blind eye to the *Chicago Manual*. But no, the smaller the outfit the more they feel the need to ape the standards of their corporate betters, and thus do traditions perpetuate themselves. I guess there's not a whole lot of room for risk in bookery even at the starvation level, where you'd think no one should give a fuck. So I've never been able to make headway with my pet notion, which is the definition of risky business. To wit: the form of a book is its superstructure and the content its substructure. What this means, to me, is that a book should be translated *before* it's been written.

But I had no way of knowing how quick this idea would come back to chomp me in the butt.

Here is a picture of a bank of swans on Lake Geneva:

8

Does it help when I hold the pictures up like that? It's hard for me to say 'Here is a picture of a bank of swans on Lake Geneva' and then not show you the picture. Oh, thanks. You're sweet. I took all these myself. Some of them aren't very good, but I need them, not to illustrate the text per se but to reinforce certain subliminal messaging that's crucial to what I'm trying to do.

Do you have any questions so far?

Huh. My favourite English writer? You mean writer in the English language, I assume. Let me first freshen your drink, because I do tend to drone on about her. Why not try a Vieux Carré?

1 OZ SINGANI 63

1 OZ COGNAC

1 OZ ANTICA FORMULA

1 BAR SPOON BÉNÉDICTINE

2 DASHES ANGOSTURA BITTERS

2 DASHES PEYCHAUD'S BITTERS

STIR ALL INGREDIENTS OVER ICE, STRAIN INTO ROCKS GLASS. NO GARNISH.

VIEUX CARRE

Deep breath. My favourite English language writer ever and anon is Sean O'Hanlon, pen name of the dead Irish author Aednat Cearbhall, who wrote *Miserogeny* in 1948, when she was twenty-seven. With a name like Aednat Cearbhall, you can understand why she chose an alias, and the world being what the world was in 1948, you can further understand why she chose a male alias, or malias if you're the kind of person who enjoys awful occasionalisms.

As Fiat Lux, whose notebooks were published in 2006 under the title *Artificial Light* (and translated by me into French and Italian), put it: 'Miserogeny [. . .] though often described as a novel, is as much an epic poem, sketchbook, series of unconnected essays, aperçus, epigrams, dicta, lists, formless only because it transcends form.'

An accurate, if unrefined and ungrammatical description.

O'Hanlon published nothing else in her brief lifetime (she died at thirty-eight, raped and murdered by her ex-husband's brother), but a posthumous unfinished volume entitled *Feeble's Diktat* was brought out in the early sixties by New Directions in the US and roundly ignored. I have first editions of both *Miserogeny* and *Feeble's Diktat*, which are the only first editions I've ever owned, or wanted to own. Neither is signed, but the internet tells me that signed copies of O'Hanlon's books don't exist and possibly never existed, their author's signature being considered of so little value while she was upright and taking nourishment that no one thought to solicit it.

Though she died nearly a half-century before I was born, I sometimes feel that, twin sister aside, O'Hanlon is the person I know and like best on our gravity-afflicted orb. No idea what she was like as a human. My affinity arises from her way with words, because either due to my vocation or to some sort of learning disorder, a person's way with words means more to me than their way with the world. Thomas Early understood. But he's dead, so that's no help.

I sometimes fantasise that under different circumstances I would have been able to turn out something as worthy as *Miserogeny*. By 'different circumstances' I mean ones in which I was born less wealthy, privileged, lazy and talentless. But that didn't happen. I'll never be Aednat Cearbhall: raped and murdered and dumped in a shallow grave in a stand of firs in her backyard, undiscovered for two weeks, by which time her ex-husband's brother had killed her ex-husband, his mother and a few other people, including himself.

There's always a bright side.

Enough about poor Aednat. Let's dive back in, like a paired couple in a bank of swans swimming in Lake Geneva.

I was twenty-five pages into my on-spec translation of *Souvenirs du triangle d'or* when I got a call from the American editor of a French writer who is absolutely Not Michel Houellebecq, who claimed that Not Houellebecq himself had requested me after reading my English version of Violette Leduc's *La Bâtarde*. Though probably the most famous French novelist alive, the writer we will call H is not a writer after my taste. He writes like a clinically depressed teenager with a limited vocabulary and a taste for misapplied Anglicisms and pop culture references that are dated before his book comes out. To tear myself away from the precise, clipped rhythms of Robbe-Grillet to tackle H's tin-eared mumble-jumble did not appeal to me. On the other hand, taking on H would mean, potentially, that I would be able to collaborate with a living author, which one always prefers to do when one can. On the newly sprouted third hand, I would be violating my rule about only translating writers I love. On the fourth hand, because I am clearly metamorphosing into some Hindu deity, which, I mean, *fine*, I can't deny that H having asked specifically for me – or so the editor said – worked on my vanity. I told his editor *OK, I'll think about it*, which is when the trouble started.

9

He wanted to meet. In person. In New York City, which is where I live but he doesn't. I was told he happened to be in town. If I wanted the job I couldn't refuse. I would have to meet Not Michel Houellebecq at a cheerless diner in what used to be called Hell's Kitchen but has since been rebranded. I would have to do this the next day at noon. I would have to pre-e-sign an e-non-disclosure agreement promising on pain of pain never to say anything about meeting H, or anything we discussed, the next day or in the future, until the end of that world in which Not Michel Houellebecq and I would meet in a diner; one among the possible worlds, it seemed, though not one that until that moment (the moment I spoke to H's editor on the phone) I would have considered probable. I would have to leave my phone at home, along with any other devices capable of recording sound that might happen to be in my possession. I was allowed a notebook and pen, but these were to be offered for inspection by any person of H's choosing during or after our meeting.

His editor didn't proscribe weapons. I nonetheless decided the next morning to leave my combat Mauser in my bedside table (I don't have a combat Mauser) before Ubering to Midtown. I walked in the door of the place, called Sammy's, and spotted H hunched over a bowl of soup in a booth whose red vinyl upholstery had seen brighter days. He wore heavy-framed glasses that disguised but did not hide his exotropic right eye; and his thick, mucusy lips smacked as he spooned in the red liquid of his soup, two-thirds of it spilling back into the bowl. His ears were crusty and rutilant, grey hairs obtruding profusely from their canals. He wore a shabby, ill-fitting olive-green herringbone blazer over an old tan sweater with black-and-white vertical stripes and dark blue trousers that were shiny at the knees. I was a little surprised to find him by himself, untended by a retinue of beefy body-guards or a waspish assistant (a hack writer deserves hack associates). I introduced myself before sliding into the booth opposite him.

He responded with a brief nod and returned to slurping his soup. I asked what manner of soup was he eating and did he recommend it, to which he said tomato and no.

It's horrible, but— he said, before insisting that we switch to English, the better to judge my competency in that language.

If I find any trace of accent, you are not correct for the job. Every French thinks he can speak English, but always he is wrong.

I agreed with H, whose opinion on this point coincided with my own, and complimented him on his perspicacity.

He shrugged again, listlessly, his wiry hair matted to his birdlike head. H has made of the Gallic shrug an instrument of precisely calibrated despair, but I don't have patience for despair.

What's the story? I asked.

The story? he said.

The new book. What's it about?

You signed the—

Yes, I signed. Don't be so fucking precious.

For the first time, H smiled. Or drew his rubbery lips back from his bony, meatless face in a caricature of a smile.

Bref: it's set in a ruined city after a disastrous war with Uruguay, he said. A beautiful woman has been found murdered in an abandoned canning factory. A secret society called the Golden Triangle exists behind a polished black door with no number and no key. The man investigating the murderer, who is sometimes also the murderer, the narrator, the victim and several other characters—

Hold on. That's the plot of *Souvenirs du triangle d'or* by Robbe-Grillet, I said.

What?

From 1978. I know for a fact because I've just begun a new English translation.

H looked at me, muddled.

That can't be right, he said.

And pitched face-forward into his soup.

10

Immediately, two sturdy (but not beefy) bodyguards I hadn't noticed, or who perhaps only now materialised from another dimension, rushed to H, grabbed him by the arms and dragged him towards the kitchen and out of sight. Before I had time to react, another man sat down in front of me.

He was around the same age as H, but deeply tanned and well dressed. Expensive haircut. Clunky Oyster Perpetual on his left wrist. He looked like a middle-aged bourgeois Parisian businessman, a type I may detest even more than hack writers. Self-assured, arrogant, but with a veneer of self-awareness that made his condescension worse.

Wonderful to meet you, he said. Sorry it had to be under such adverse conditions.

Is he OK? What happened?

I had lapsed into French, hearing how heavy his accent in English was.

He shook his head vigorously. I lived five years in New York one time, he said. My English is fluent.

Who are you? I asked.

He smiled and offered his hand, which I shook wet-ragly. You will find this hard to believe, but I am H. The *real* H.

I find that hard to believe, I said.

It started as a *blague*, a joke, more than twenty years ago. I never want to do readings or book signings, I hate those things, they're horrible. I have an idea: that I can find a big, big loser to impersonate me. I find *him*.

He nodded to the kitchen door through which the bodyguards had dragged the other H.

And you managed to keep that a secret from everyone, I said.

I'm good at keeping the secrets.

What about what's-his-name, the *type* who just passed out in his tomato soup?

I pay him well. He knows where his butter – which side of the bread . . .

I'll need to see some ID, I said.

I can do this, he said. I can show you ID until the sun jumps over the moon, but it has no use. Passport, driving licence, *carte d'identité*, *carte vitale*, these are easily imitated.

He went for his wallet. I waved it away.

What happened to the, uh, the *other* you?

His name is H, too. That's good, right? You can call him H.

OK. What happened to H?

He leaned forward to favour me with his intense French gaze. We are in a situation. I can trust you?

Sure.

For years H has many bad habits. Drinking, eating, smoking, everything. The doctors tell him, I tell him, but he does not listen. I know this is coming. I don't know when, I don't know where.

I looked at him quizzically.

Crise cardiaque, he said. And not the first. I don't think that this time he will make it.

How can you be sure? I said.

I just know. I look in his eyes in the morning, I say, *H, you don't look good*, blah blah blah, he shrug like: nothing. This is why I follow him here, and make my people ready, too.

I took a beat to digest what the insipid Parisian was telling me. I sipped water from the plastic glass a waiter had deftly slipped onto the Formica in front of me.

So it's game over? I said. No more H, no more H novels, no more gravy train.

I am reliably informed there will be a posthumous work of grand proportions. He smiled broadly.

I didn't at that time notice that his French accent had slipped, that he had spoken not just articulately but well, with a hint of Oxbridge. Much the way I sound, though five years in New York has flattened my vowels. Yes, I went to St Belinda's College for Wayward Girls in Oxford. Had to do something after my bitch twin sister stole my life.

What was that business where he was telling me the plot of the new book but it was recycled Robbe-Grillet?

H2 (as I decided at this moment to call him) laughed.

I do my homework. Well, I do not, but I have people who do this. I know you are working on a translation of *Souvenirs du triangle d'or*. So I tell H the plot. He has never read this book. It was a bit of *fon*. (The French accent was back.) He has not read my new book.

Why not? I asked.

Because it isn't written.

Something about this was a bit fishy. Something about this is a bit fishy, I said.

You like sushi? H2 said. Have dinner with me. Tonight. I know the *best* place.

If you haven't written the new book, why meet with a translator?

I think you know the answer, Ms Salomon.

I don't, actually.

I think you do.

Not a clue.

Well then. It will be an adventure.

He got up, nodded at the two sturdy but not beefy body-guards who had returned from the kitchen and were seated at the counter, as inconspicuous as Not Michel Houellebecq face down in tomato soup, and marched out the door of the diner.

A car will pick you up at eight-thirty from your apartment, he said.

11

He left a business card by my water glass. It was a white rect-
angle, empty except for a French cellphone number in matt
black lettering. When I went for my phone it was already
buzzing in my handbag. That same number was calling.

You were told not to bring your phone. It was H2.

I forgot, I said.

I was lying to him. I don't go anywhere without my phone.
And I don't take instructions from either H.

I'm having a dress sent to your apartment. I will be happy
if you wear it to dinner tonight.

A dress, I said. For heaven's sake. First of all, I don't wear
dresses. It's not my deal. Second of all, as a matter of principle, I will not be clothed or unclothed by any person except
at my own time and choosing.

Angelica would wear the guy's dress. She's always wearing
some guy's dress. To premieres, to parties, to the shopping
mall. We haven't spoken in years, so the bulk of my AI
(Angelica Info) comes from my parents or what I read on
the gossip sites whenever I visit gossip sites, which is not
often. Maybe five or ten times a day. When my parents try
to tell me what twin sis is up to, I shut them down quickly;
but I surreptitiously track her all the time, which fills me with

such self-loathing that I delete my browser history every week in case I die or someone boosts my computer and somehow it gets back to Angelica that I'm obsessed with her. Which I am not, except insofar as I am.

She's the chief reason dresses are not my deal. I wear jeans and a T-shirt most days. I look good in whatever, and jeans and a T-shirt are easy. As long as they're obscenely overpriced designer T-shirts and jeans. And silk underwear, because I adore anything silk. My sheets are silk, my bedspread is silk, my pyjamas are silk, my sleep mask is silk. Organic, ethically sourced from ideologically stainless worms, 20 momme minimum. I make no apologies for my sericophilia. I perhaps *should* make apologies for the immense unmerited funds at my disposal, but if you're looking for fair, as a friend said to me recently, you're in the wrong universe.

I donate an ample sum from my ample sums every year to a Tibetan Buddhist temple in the Auvergne in central France called Dhagpo Kundreul Ling, partly for tax reasons, partly out of embarrassment, and partly because I'm genuinely attracted to certain Tibetan Buddhist traditions – though I'm certainly no Buddhist, Tibetan or otherwise. In return for all that dosh, I'm permitted to take as many long or short retreats in the Pende Ling hermitage as I want. The traditional retreat is three years. I haven't worked up to that yet. I've done the three-month retreat twice, and a fistful of week-long or two-week-long or month-long retreats. During the retreat you don't speak to anyone, not even during the communal meals, not even when you're working in the bamboo garden. It's glorious. In exchange for my money and a token application of labour I get to unbend my vigil wrt the world's endlessly obstreperous *maculae*. I call that a bargain. The rest of the time you meditate. You're not supposed to read, but I read anyway. The lama doesn't like it, but he doesn't forbid it.

Here is a picture of the temple:

I love the way it's been set down or possibly raised up in the Middle of Nowhere, France, as out of place as I must look in the hermitage. There's also a nunnery four kilometres away where female followers of the path shut themselves up conventually for life. I have always assumed I would end up there. My will leaves everything to the temple. Does that make you feel any better about me? I guess it makes me feel better about me.

I don't wear make-up or jewellery or ornaments of any kind. Not because I don't need any of these things, but because I don't care and am lazy, in that order. The world is lucky when I wash my hair, which I do less frequently than I care to admit. I should issue a press release every time I condescend to lather, rinse, repeat my tresses with tea tree-oil-infused sodium sulphate. I also more than a little despise the hygienic routines of the washed masses. Americans are obsessed with showering. I don't get it. Showering is actively awful for you. For your skin, your hair, your health, the planet. The planet's fucked. But your body? You have to live with that.

When I got back to my apartment there was a package waiting with the doorman. Whose name I believe is Stan. I tip him a few hundred dollars every Christmas so that he doesn't hold it against me that I don't know his name.

Is it Stan? It's Max? Are you sure? Well, you're a nicer person than I am, Juno. That's not saying much, but it is saying something.

I took the package up to my apartment and opened it. In it I discovered an ultramarine Chanel sheath gown with a slight flare at the bottom that tapered at the heels. I tried it on. I looked amazing. I decided what the hell, can't hurt to wear a dress once in a while.

12

Before going to meet H2, I flushed the wax out of my ears with carbamide peroxide and a soft rubber bulb, as I have to do whenever I venture out in public where loud conversation is likely to occur in an enclosed space. I have a hearing problem, partly because I did so much cocaine in my early twenties that I damaged everything inside me, and partly because I spent a lot of that coked-up time in hellishly loud nightclubs dancing long past dawn.

After flushing out my ears, I thought, as I always do, that I could hear a little better, but my tinnitus, which is louder than the hum of my *frigo*, had (as it always does) if anything grown stronger; at night when my apartment is quiet and no cars jostle through the street five storeys below all I can hear is a persistent hiss. If I dwell on the hiss it drives me to distraction, and if I ignore it — I can't ignore it because my brain knows I'm trying to ignore it and redoubles its efforts to bring it to my attention. Like not thinking about elephants, to use the classic example (*vide* Pliny *Nat. His.* 7.1), a thing once noticed will loom gargantua in your pantagruel no matter how you try to rabelais. Hence my chronic insomnia, which is taking hours off my end-of-life; not that I care what happens to me at the end any more than I did at the beginning.

In the end the bad guys win. The bad guys always win. In movies, after the bad guys are defeated, you know they're not gone for good. They've retreated, probably somewhere nicer than where the good guys are, and will heal their grievous wounds and nurse their grievous grievances until such time as they feel spunky enough to renew the pro forma battle.

The world's bad guys are hydra-headed. It's no use going back in your time machine and killing just one. Kill baby Hitler and what? Anti-Semitism disappears from Europe? It's hard to conjure up anything worse than what did happen, but I'm betting someone would find a way. Maybe Stalin solo would have been worse. He had a lot of ideas how to kill people. Kill Hitler, and Stalin's got a free hand in Europe. It's no good killing Stalin either, because then Hitler reaches Moscow, Britain sues for peace, and – it's the stuff of science fiction. My larger point is that you, you personally, are guilty of every crime that's been committed or will be committed by any single member of the human formicary. No one is innocent, no infant or elderly saint. You are born guilty. Not through Original Sin, because if there was an original sin, it was the Big Bang, and no one knows (yet) why that happened or (yet) how to expiate it. Over the slow course of evolution, from wherever we started to whomever we've become, we haven't changed. We're the same selfish, vicious, uncaring, cruel, vain, greedy, sublunary creeps who lumbered out of the savannah looking for lower-hanging fruit.

The world's bad guys are you. You, yourself, are a terrible person. You are without ruth. I can tell that to your face without having met you. Kill Hitler and you become Hitler. This is easy. This is Being Human for beginners. This is proved every time any person inflicts pain on any noun. What one can do, all can do, and what one does, all do. An animal can sacrifice itself to protect its young. It's an inbuilt instinct to preserve the species. It's not courage. It doesn't take courage to kill or let yourself be killed to save someone else. It takes humanity to plan and execute the murder of dozens, hundreds, thousands, millions of other people. It takes humanity to organise killing on a mass scale, and to justify those killings. It takes humanity to give orders, and humanity to follow them. It takes humanity to serve, to be obedient, to pray, to screw everything up. The impulse towards irony — the irrational, to radically oversimplify, because I am nothing if not radically oversimple (but this is not the time for jokes) — is the bit worth saving wrt humanity, the quirk that defines us. The impulse towards irony lets us drive our Tesla at one hundred miles per hour into a brick wall knowing full well that we will die, not because we want to die, but out of bloody-minded contrariness. We can say the sky is cotton-red and the trees are ripe-blue despite the evidence of our senses. We can choose not to believe in imaginary numbers, or to believe that stepping on a crack will break your mother's back. That's it. That's our hope. That is our glistering candle in the blowy darkness of evil. Not good. Not God. *The impulse towards irony.* That's our secret weapon, the more effective because the more secret.

13

My name is Vanessa Salomon. At *lycée* I once introduced myself in Latin class as Vanessa Salome, but no one noticed except my teacher, a pallid beldam with few of her original teeth and fewer original ideas. For whatever reason she took a liking to me. She let me study at my own pace, ahead of the others, except for Angelica, who lapped me whenever my attention flagged, which was often.

Mme Franck smoked a pipe, which though it might seem eccentric was in fashion among the distaff staff at that time, and her rookery always smelled of cherry tobacco. I have affectionate recollections of smoky hours spent puzzling over the *Aeneid* while she worked her way through Dante, despite not knowing Italian, using her sturdy, unspectacular Latin as a Virgil. She was meant to be teaching me, but I didn't need much teaching; just a spare hand on occasion climbing out of a few thorny patches where the profusion of ablatives that PV Maro had planted to preserve the integrity of his dactylic hexameters had trapped me in a spiky hug.

I didn't know it then, but I suffer from a condition where my body produces a *superflu* of adrenaline, putting me in a constant state of anticipatory excitement no matter the sitch wrt stimuli. I floated through my *lycée* years in a haze only half hash-induced, and retain from that period indistinct impressions more than specific memories. Memorandum (with apologies to John Aubrey): the smell of newly cut grass or the sight of a maple bud swelling open infallibly transports me to Mme Franck's office. I spent more time gazing out of her window at the schoolyard, listening to the birds complain and the occasional musical chirp of a bullied kid hung from a pole by his underwear, than I did fearing the gift-bearing Greeks. Whatever I have retained of the *Aeneid* is by sense-association. The scent of jasmine induces visions of Dido's sad altar, the sight of dandelions a Trojan Horse that in my mind's eye could canter and buck like Paul Duchamp, the best goalkeeper in school history. His hands were sticky with sweat and other substances when we lay on the pitch at dusk engaged in amorous *ébats* for less time than I would have liked.

Mme Franck was a decent Latinist but a poor teacher. She had that schoolmastery habit, handed down from Mr Partridge in Henry Fielding's satire, of quoting bits from our Latin primer whether these were *à propos* or not. Horace's hoary *Non quivis videt inmodulata poemata iudex* was a favourite, possibly because of its wide applicability, but more likely because it had inscribed itself on the smooth slopes of her cerebellum through overuse. No matter: between us A and I could solve almost any syntactical riddle, and did, and the foundation provided by Latin emerged over the years as well suited to my House of Languages.

It's all bootless, all quite bootless. It boots not. Like herding the wind, as Qohelet says in Robert Alter's wonderful translation. When I'm gone nothing will remain of what I did or said or felt or thought. Not a jot.

The prospect of oblivion delights me more than I can say.

14

He was there when I arrived. H2 was a big fan of sushi, and had strong opinions about which were the best sushi restaurants. I'm mostly vegan, except when I'm not, and sushi has never been one of my fave food groups; further, I have found that the more exclusive/expensive a sushi joint is, the less I incline to enjoy it. I'm not sure why this should be the case, possibly more to do with the clientele (ignoring each other while doomscrolling through their social media feeds) than with the food itself, which, if you like that kind of thing, is typically exquisite. This one was vertiginously exclusive/expensive, and I expected to hate it. Its one plus was a surprisingly ample wine list.

But instead of wine, I ordered a Bolivian 63:

2 OZ SINGANI 63
.75 OZ LEMON JUICE
.75 OZ SIMPLE SYRUP
CHAMPAGNE
LEMON TWIST

SHAKE FIRST THREE INGREDIENTS WITH
ICE, THEN STRAIN INTO A FLUTE GLASS.
TOP WITH CHAMPAGNE AND GARNISH
WITH A LEMON TWIST.

BOLIVIAN 63

Am fairly sure H2 was wearing the same suit; and he hadn't shaved. His eyes were as blue as any I've seen, barring those false contact-lens colours you sometimes encounter. He wore a blue dress shirt with white cuffs, blue to accentuate the eyes, white cuffs rolled back rather than closed and linked to accentuate that the shirt was expensive but that he didn't care. His collar, unbuttoned because tieless, was lined on the inside with narrow rose-and-white stripes. It was a good shirt. The shirt was his best feature. Inasmuch as I could judge through the tears his numinous waft of expensive cologne brought to my eyes. He was on a call when I arrived, wearing wireless earbuds and speaking in rapid Parisian French (slangy Franglish) to someone about travel arrangements. He smiled when he saw me and got up, gestured for me to sit down, held up one finger and mouthed *sorry* as he wrapped up the call.

You look amazing in that dress, he said, when he had hung up. I mean, wow.

Yes, thank you, I replied.

No use denying the obvious. Every eye had followed me across the dimly lit dining room. Every eye has followed me my whole life, but when I make an effort, it's like H2 said, *Wow*. You get used to it. Sometimes you take it for granted, and sometimes you misinterpret it, and some people (my favourite kind) have no interest in superficial beauty and are unmoved by my genetic gifts. The only man I ever loved — keeping in mind the heteroclite nature of the word *love*, as Mr Powell's Delavaquerie would likely warn — told me often that I was the most sightly creature on earth, but did not mean it in the usual sense.

He thought me beautiful for reasons unconnected to my physical splendour, which is one reason why I loved him. He's dead. I killed him.

15

I had no idea what food to order, so I let H2 do it. I ate, self-consciously, whatever the server brought us. Because I've never been enamoured of any food that requires the use of chopsticks, I've never been able to master them. Which doesn't prevent me from using them. Men enjoy watching women eat sloppily. Because everything to them is oriented towards the gratification of their primary sense organ, or penis in the vernacular, a woman eating sloppily reminds them of fellatio.

I've long since ceased to care what any member – of any assigned or chosen gender or sexual preference or racial identity or socio-economic background or tribal ideology or even just skin colour (from sable to calcareous on the cosmetological spectrum) – of this human race thinks about how I look or how I act or what I do or say. That sounds grandiose. Or I hope it does. But it's true, and never more true than when I am conscious that what I'm doing could be construed as sexually provocative.

To his credit (I guess), though I'm sure H2 noticed what was going on with my mouth and the slippery fish and the chopsticks, he didn't stare unduly nor did he make the kind of crass comment any other bourgeois Parisian would have made on that occasion. In retrospect I think this was because his self-absorption was so complete it rarely allowed for observation or analysis of anyone else, that is to say the existence of other people in general and the actions of specific other people.

He ran down the list of my greatest translating hits like ticking boxes on an exam he could easily pass, having himself designed the thing. I acknowledged with offhand grace his praise of my work, because why protest when someone professes to rate something you know is not good (because you did it yourself), just as why protest when someone slates something you know is good (for the same reason). MSM reviews of the books I translate rarely mention the quality of the translation. At least, that's what I figure. I don't read reviews of the books I translate. I extrapolate my assumption from occasionally reading reviews of books other people have translated, noting that, except in cases where the translator is herself a prominent author or the book is a 'classic' being reissued with an overhauled translation, the reviewer rarely touches on the quality of the translation. Specialist or well-funded highbrow journals take particular trouble to enlist reviewers conversant both with the original language and the art of translation, but those are the exceptions in the dominion over which I rule. Gosh, this crown is heavy.

Some of my translations are better than others, sure. I work harder on books that deserve my full attention, and I'm careless with dross. *Souvenirs du triangle d'or* is an example of a book that I'm planning to work hard on. H's book is an example of one I had figured I'd do cursorily. Though when I put my mind to it I'm probably in the upper *tierce* of translators, I'm not always gripped with a craving to put my mind to it.

When H2 praised my limpid rendering of Hemingway's *A Farewell to Arms* into French, I had to quell the urge to laugh. I did that translation as a favour. Hemingway is trash, a chump, and my translation was faithful to his talent. Anyone who would aver otherwise is either blowing smoke up my ass (*Have you ever had anyone actually blow smoke up your ass? Like straight up your asshole? I have; it's not unpleasant*) or taking the piss, or clueless. It's been my experience that most readers are clueless. Present company excepted.

16

Men are so predictable. This is a horrible generalisation from a person who prides herself on her allergy to generalisations. Still: what acculturated impulse encourages them to assume anyone wants to hear the story of their lives? After he finished a cursory ramble through my resumé, H2 started in on himself. He related in prodigious detail how he'd been born the only child of a divorced man in his thirties (there were rumours of an older stepbrother but he never found out more), how his mother had died when he was young, how his father was some big industrialist, the head of a chemical company in France, and how he'd been expected to toe the family line, but that when he went off to university he realised that his vocation (he used the word vocation) was for writing fiction.

I soon stopped paying attention. Origin stories are profoundly uninteresting to me. This might seem hypocritical, but *croyez-moi*, I'd decidedly rather not tell you a smidge, the merest fleck, about myself or how I grew up or why I turned to translating after my bitch twin sister stole my life. I'd rather never mention my bitch twin sister again. I admit I get a charge every time I write 'bitch twin sister'. It satisfies something small and mean inside me that I'd rather not investigate but acknowledge does exist, as I acknowledge slugs exist; but I don't go around lifting up rocks and rotten logs.

There was something about a woman not his wife — H2 kept spouting cetaceously about a woman not his wife. There's always something about a woman not his wife when French men tell you their story, however potted. It's a show of ersatz honesty, letting you know that they are vulnerable to hurt, that their heart has been broken; but life goes on, and you may as well let them fuck you in the ass they just blew smoke up because none but transitory pleasures remain, wretch that they are, their skeleton a broken xylophone on which you can only play *Clair de lune*, out of tune, better now than soon.

When I was eighteen I only used to date older men, and many of them turned out to be married, which was fine, because marriage is a joke and monogamy a hoax, or perhaps I've got that backwards. True love exists at the bottom of a bottle of Pomerol, in the form of sediment. You don't drink the sediment. You can, but it'll mess up your digestion. That's what I think of true love.

The older, married men thing turned out to be a phase. Too much histrionics with older, married men, who in that respect are so unlike older, married women. I was still in mourning, so I was unlikely tonight to respond to any human creature's overtures, much less this one's, but I don't think H2 was trying to seduce me. I'm sure he would have fucked me in the ass given the chance, and tbh I didn't feel strongly one way or other about him fucking me in the ass. Don't know why I had this fixed idea that he liked buggery, it's just, some guys look like ass-fuckers. If he were to fuck me, I guarantee that however we started off doing it we'd end up with his dick in my ass.

As it turned out we never did end up with his dick in my ass, but, as I say, it was a matter of little interest.

17

Your father must have been in a flap when you told him you didn't want to be a chemical company executive but a writer, I said, to be polite.

No, he was not in a flap. Because I never told him. Today I am the CEO of the company he ran. But it's a long story, and I don't want to bore you.

Too late!

It is partly for this reason, he said, that I had the idea of hiring him to represent me at readings and interviews and so on. That way I could continue to write books, but also to pursue my regular job, at which it happens I have some innate talent, and so travelled up the corporate ladder in predictable ways. Today I have a private jet, bodyguards, a summer house in Cap Ferret, a big house in Paris, an apartment in New York, et cetera et cetera. But these are not all from the royalties to my books, much of this is paid for by the company, Chimico. Have you tried this otoro? It's excellent.

He held out a piece of pink tuna suspended at the end of his chopsticks. I was meant to take the bait, so to speak. I did. And swallowed.

Yes, tremendous, excellent, I said. I washed the slimy sea vermin down my gullet with a swish of Singani sour.

But how do you find the time to write the books and run the company? I asked.

He sighed. That has become increasingly difficult, he said. I am sad that H has died, but in another way I am not sad, because I will have more free time.

After you finish the last book, I said.

That is what I want to talk to you about. I am aware of your theories regarding translation. Correct me if I am mistaken, but do you not believe that the ideal translation would take place before the book in question has even been written?

He shuffled through some papers. Yes. Here it is. In Chapter 7, towards the end.

This was more than doing his homework. This was invasion of privacy. This was mind reading, or something worse. But I'm cool, so I played it me.

You have me there, I said. But what makes you think that I would do this for you?

H2 smiled the broad, shit-eating Gallic smile I had already come to hate, the smile that I'm sure has charmed a thousand, maybe more, women and (why not?) men out of their clothes and into his bed.

You're already doing it. *Alea iacta est*, as the Romans would say.

If I refuse?

Tant pis. I think you will not refuse. From what I understand, you enjoy a challenge. From what I understand, you have not been much engaged with your work lately. The Robbe-Grillet translation is, I believe, on spec. It was not commissioned by a publisher.

Someone, somewhere will want to publish it. I'm very good.

I do not doubt this.

I'll think on it. I'll have a think.

Good. We are agreed, he said.

I decided to make a semi-dramatic exit, without replying, because I've seen this done in movies and always enjoy it. I pushed back my chair, got up, walked out. Didn't look back. Didn't have to. I knew he was leering after me. The air, when I hit the street, was pendulous with humidity. My breath made little ghosts. I hailed a cab. The night was cold and dark with smeary jets of neon reflected on the wet street.

In the cab, I slumped in the seat and cried, noiselessly.

18

A tiny part of me was flattered that anyone would take the trouble to invade my privacy. It's hard to root up my truffles. I'm not on social media, because social media is the quickest path towards a weeks-long depression caused by the omnipresence of my bitch twin sister in a sphere I was born to dominate, and by sphere I mean the world as filtered through the internet, and by dominate I mean dominate. More, I don't understand the impulse every other nobody feels to volunteer secrets to an uncaring nest of vipery spies. Or 'friends', as people call them. I don't have friends in the first place, whether virtual or actual, and I do not like to divulge information anent myself. Have you read Diderot's *Les Bijoux indiscrets*? That's how I see the current culture of sharing. A bunch of talkative twats.

I've never had use for friends, and vice versa. I am not a likeable person. I understand and accept that fact. But other people are not likeable people. It's clear in the abstract that humans are social animals, that nothing can be taken wholly in isolation, that everything and everyone is connected via fungal mycelium and the mucous membranes of certain highly coloured poisonous frogs in what's left of the Amazon rainforest and the rocks, man, all of the rocks, alive with crystalline vibrations, dancing like pinwheel-eyed Burning Men in every one of the ten or eleven or, wait now, it's thirteen possible dimensions – but yeah, no. I don't like people. I don't like their shapes and sizes, the odours they give off, the lies they tell, their stubby toes, scaly scalps, greasy faces, the glaucous droop of their heavy-lidded dull-as-sugar eyes, their limp pricks and dusty cunts, the squeak of their rubber-soled shoes on polished wood, their breath, the sound of their breath, their hot breath on my neck, anything they say out loud, even to tell me something I desperately need to hear.

But you can't get away from them, or they from you, not forever. You can't think them away. You can't protect the keep of your castle from the besieging hordes, because the hordes built the castle and you owe them for the keep. It's not yours to defend. Anything you do not own outright or that doesn't directly contribute to your survival I call nostalgia, the worst of the nine deadly sins, and should be slated for destruction, virtual and/or actual. Francesca Woodman once wrote about the *pell-mell erasing of all these delicate things*. I don't know what that means, but it fits my current mood.

We're all getting older, and as we age the biological imperative to replicate ourselves competes with the collective unconscious urge to destroy ourselves and our environment. That's the joke. That's the laugh at the end of the procreative yelp: the primitive ugh of some prick shooting his load into some quim's eager bin: followed by a process that not all the king's horses nor all the king's men can unsee or unbend: coming comes undone and becomes.

Kids are people too. And I hate people.

19

All these disconnected ramblings had apparently been uncovered in the course of H2's unauthorised recce through my private musings, so I had to sit there and listen as he read from my dossier.

I was appalled, but he looked at least as discomfited.

I do not understand. You hate children?

The idea of children. That they exist. I'm not good with that.

But what has this to do with our agreement?

I don't know. You're the one who insisted on reading it.

And you hate sex? And nostalgia?

I hate nostalgia for sex. I hate romanticising. But most of all, as you just announced to the rest of the restaurant, I hate people. In general, and, generally, specific people. Right now, you're at the top of that list.

We won't argue, he said. Let's proceed.

Keeping in mind that I have not yet consented to your proposal. Which means that there's a sense in which your proposal is, at least at this point, assault.

You will find when you return home an envelope that has been left with your doorman. The envelope will contain a first-class Air France ticket leaving tomorrow afternoon from JFK for Paris. Upon arrival in Paris you will be met by a driver.

Sure.

The driver will take you to my house in— I do not like to say where. It is just outside Paris. What food do you prefer? I will instruct my cook to prepare it.

You have your own cook?

My wife does not enjoy to make food, he said.

You have your own wife?

And two children. Little girls. Seven and ten. No. Eight and eleven. No. Seven and ten.

You are number six.

That is a reference to *The Prisoner*, a sixties British television series that has developed a cult following.

If you say so, French dude.

My children's names are Mary and Temple.

Les pauvres gosses. As to dietary predilections, I'm vegan.

You just ate sushi.

But I didn't enjoy it. *Typically*, I'm vegan. No meat, no eggs, no cheese, no butter, no dairy of any kind.

That presents a problem.

Stop pretending you care about my coqueral needs. I'll eat whatever. Seared foie gras on a bed of caviar sitting in lobster bisque. An entire cow. Let's talk money.

You have no need of money.

Not a matter of need. A question of want.

There are limits—

No. There are no limits. I want five hundred thousand euros. Half up front, half on delivery. I already signed the NDA but I will agree to any constraints on the disclosure of information you make available to me. I won't even tell my parents.

You can tell your parents. I would prefer it.

Why?

This means they won't worry. You will be required to travel a lot and at times will be unreachable by phone or internet.

Why will I be required to travel and why will I be unreachable?

You will travel because I must travel, and you must accompany me. And you will be unreachable because I wish you to be unreachable. For five hundred thousand euros I expect to be able to put in place certain strictures that will ensure you are fully engaged with the work.

Fine. I'll tell my parents. You probably already know this, but my sister—

The shadow of an emotion darted across his face, but I couldn't tell which one. It was too transient.

Yes, I know about your sister, he said.

If I tell my parents, they'll probably tell my sister. Even if I tell them not to tell my sister.

I don't have a problem with them telling your sister.

She's not known for her discretion.

He sipped his freshly delivered Singani Sour, another round of which had appeared at our table without my having noticed. I took hold of mine and hemi-downed it in a single gulp.

Do you think anyone will believe such a ludicrous story? he asked. That you are translating the latest novel by a famous French writer before it has been written?

What people believe doesn't interest me, I said.

His eyes flashed bluely in the mellow ruby light of the restaurant.

Alors. The money will be wired to your account tomorrow.

Super.

He stood up, rolled his neck round the pink-lined collar of his shirt, yawned widely.

And now you must excuse me. The dinner is taken care of, and you should feel free to order anything else you wish. I have not slept in two days.

I waved him away from the table as if I were dismissing a servant.

Run along, H2.

What?

I can't call you Not Michel Houellebecq. It's too absurd. And the other one came first so he's H1. You're H2.

He nodded. H2, he said. I like that. It sounds like a tall mountain.

The alcohol was starting to go to my head.

Or the second album by a progressive rock band, I said. Anyway, there's something Alpine in the matter of you.

He bowed. Slightly, but still. He fucking bowed. And left.

Maybe it's the rank cologne, I said to no one in particular.

20

When the plane touched down at Roissy I woke from what felt like a forever sleep. I'd dosed myself with Klonopin an hour before take-off. Sometimes it keeps me out for the full eight hours it takes to go from JFK to CDG, sometimes for only an hour. Depends a lot on what you've eaten, which is true for so much in life. This time I'd knocked myself out for the duration, which is grand except for the part where one wakes up dehydrated as if one has drunk all the sand in the Gobi desert, which effect was particularly embellished when one was hungover as the result of overbevvying Singani 63 the night before the flight (check!).

The promised driver was waiting by the customs exit. He introduced himself as Alexandre and asked if I needed help with my luggage. I nodded at my rucksack and told him that was it, that was my luggage, so no, I didn't need help with my luggage. Alexandre was wearing a chauffeur's uniform, or an ill-fitting grey suit. I was wearing clingy black sweatpants, a white T-shirt, and a thin grey hoodie, and had oversized sunglasses on despite the weather, which was as grey as Alexandre's suit. I'm sure that despite feeling haggard and foggy I looked hot. I could tell by Alexandre's reaction when he checked out my ass as he ushered me through the terminal door and towards his grey Mercedes. I let it slide because everyone checks out my ass. Including me. Sometimes I spend significant segments of the day or night checking out my ass in the mirror on the inside door of my bedroom closet at home. It's time well spent.

What I could not tolerate, however, was his transcendently lame chit-chat during the interminable drive to wherever-the-fuck, France. *How was your flight what's the weather like in New York I've been there five times myself I love that city if I get enough money I would love to move there but also to Los Angeles don't you love Los Angeles the weather is so great there what part of France are you from* and on and on and on. The guy was relentless, despite the fact I never answered a single question. Some people can sustain a conversation by themselves for hours, and I am a magnet for these interesting types, particularly when I'm hungover. My usual countermeasure is to put my earbuds in and turn up the Quartetto Italiano recording of Beethoven's late string quartets, but my phone's battery had died sometime during my flight-long blackout, so my back-up plan of feigning sleep was deployed, with limited success.

By the time we arrived at wherever-the-fuck and pulled into the long semicircle gravel driveway and up to the steps of what I'm sure H2 would call his *hôtel particulier*, but I would call a large and tastelessly designed suburban faux chateau – lacking only machicolations, or more properly *mâchicoulis*, through which to pour boiling oil on *hoi polloi* – Alexandre had given up his attempt at conversation and was instead happily humming along to some trite French pop song on

Chérie FM (*Toutes vos chansons préférées, non stop*). I'm of the opinion that all Parisian men are isophiles, though they might not themselves be aware of it. The world would be a far better place if my opinion were fact.

21

H2 greeted me at the top of the stone steps, champagne flute
in hand. He wasn't wearing a jacket, and had on a pair of
new-looking blue jeans, but his shirt was either the same or
identical to the shirt he had worn in New York, and he was
wearing polished wingtips. He looked like a French bourgeois
trying too hard to dress down.

Welcome, welcome, please come in! he said, handing me
the champagne and relieving me of my rucksack, which he
set on a chair in a room just to the left of the entrance,
where I saw a grand piano, a sofa and a few easy chairs.
There were bookshelves, but (curiously, given one of his
putative professions) not many books. A ficus plant in a
brass pot.

I'm so glad to see you, he said, beaming, skin creasing at
the corners of his eyes. Let me show you around.

I allowed myself to be led through a succession of unin-
spiring rooms, some of which were, e.g., painted pale blue
with ivory wainscoting, furnitured by wan seventies-era
chairs and tables and globe lamps. More pots with more
plants: moth orchid, anthurium, African violets, an improbable palm. The floors were cherrywood brown throughout
and polished to a gloss.

We arrived eventually at double doors leading to the back garden, or more properly to a concrete deck rimmed by a nondescript balustrade leading down on both the left and right sides to the back garden, which was itself encircled by the boles of immature trees, mostly fir with some lime trees and oaks. The showpiece of the garden was a life-size bronze bull in full gallop at the far end. I hated it. I hated everything about the mock François 1er architecture, the turfy, close-cropped lawn, the tennis court tucked behind the house. A hard court. In France, the land of red clay, a hard court. The ignominy of it.

But I hated it most of all because I recognised it. Growing up, I spent many afternoons in houses like this one, at friends of my parents who thought it either irresponsible or too expensive to bring up their children in the great wen of Paris. Angelica and I were often dropped off without warning after school at one or another of our ostensible friends' residences, our own desires unconsulted and our subsequent complaints ignored. We spent hours performing elaborate apotropaic rites over our play dates' corpses after we had killed them with the compact hatchets we always carried for that purpose. Or we played hide-and-seek until dusk, when we were called inside to eat dinner, or to play card games until one of our parents or a hireling deputised to the task came in our sleek black Volvo to pick us up.

Isn't it wonderful? asked H2, gesturing from the balcony. You would never know you're minutes away from the city centre.

When do we eat? I said.

Here's a picture taken from the window of a crumbling chateau in the Val-d'Oise:

22

The dinner was as you would expect. Charcuterie, pâté and bread, followed by soup, followed by a first course consisting of trout filleted and drowned in butter and cream, followed by duck, with various side dishes, just one of which was identifiable as containing exclusively vegetable matter, followed by cheese, followed by crème brûlée. All accompanied by wine that was continually replenished from a crystal decanter by the attentive waiting staff H2 employed.

I met his wife, who was called Caro, or that's how he introduced her to me, so that's what I called her too. (Caro is the diminutive form of Caroline; in France diminutives are regularly employed to address children and strippers.) Her hair was dyed blonde and pulled back from her face in a severe ponytail, and she was dressed, for reasons I hope made sense to someone, in equestrian clothes for dinner: jodhpurs, riding boots, white blouse and close-fitting velvet-green jacket trimmed with black satin. She looked to be in her mid-thirties, and her breasts looked to be three years old, judging from their determinedly upward trajectory and relative immobility. But I would have had to feel them to be certain.

As I watched her sip her soup I idly wondered what it would be like to fistfuck Caro, whether she would be loud and unruly or more quietly passionate, whether she would put up much resistance to the idea, how hard it would be to work my long-fingered hand into her cunt. Because she had given birth twice I expected there would be some pliability to her vagina, unless she'd had a caesarean both times, which was unlikely.

I visualised drugging Caro, laying her out on the dinner table, and using a steak knife to slit her trousers from her calf to her crotch, through her underwear, exposing her pubis, continuing to cut upwards, through her shirt, to reveal her breasts. Rubbing ice on her large round nipples to make them erect. Lifting the curve of her breasts to look for surgical incisions or scars, purely to satisfy my curiosity, because I don't care one way or another. Kneading her breasts like checking for a dud avocado. Tying her unresisting hands above her head with ropes to the hanging chandelier in the middle of the table, and whipping her back with a riding crop until her white skin was cross-hatched with red stripes, and the red stripes oozed thick blood, at which point I would crawl onto the table and lick the gore from her back, smearing it over my face, pressing myself against her naked flesh, finally severing the ropes that held her and watching her flop back down on the table, at which point she would wake, dazed, to see my blood-smeared face grinning wildly at her.

I found the duck rather dry.

Sorry. I got a little carried away. One thing about Robbe-Grillet is that he was by most standard units of measure a pervy pervert. He was into bondage and little girls, just for starters. Some of that may have rubbed off on me, and if it's offensive, I apologise. Unless you enjoyed it, in which case I do not apologise. I have to warn you, Juno, things are only going to get weirder from here on out. If at any time you're uncomfortable, you have only to raise your hand, and you'll be punished, I mean of course excused.

[Section deleted because some things are private.]

23

The children weren't at dinner, presumably because it was late, but I had been introduced earlier. They were fastidiously polite, both of them, trained to *faire les bises* with friends and strangers alike. They had been taken upstairs by the nanny to do their homework before bed. I assume they had homework. You can never be sure when it's a school holiday in France, because every other week is a school holiday. You think I'm kidding, go download the French holidays calendar for whatever year this is. They have so many school holidays they have to divide the country up into different districts so that all the kids aren't on holiday at once. Which wouldn't be a problem except that when the kids go on holiday, the parents do as well, so the whole bloody country's on holiday most of the time. That's why they had to do the district thing.

When I'm president of France, which I will be on the day France elects the anarchist-green-hunting coalition to a parliamentary majority, I will have not only the regions and the departments and the districts and the towns and villages and hamlets and households and men and women efficiently censused and taxed, but every single child bar-coded and colour-sorted, and assigned not to their birth family but to the family that's best able to keep them out of my sight for the duration of my presidency, which in the absence of term limits (abolished by me) is likely to be the rest of my unnatural life.

After dinner we went into the room with the grand piano, which you could call a lounge or salon. The wallpaper was raw umber flocked in a recurring triangular pattern from the baseboard; then a delicate duck-egg-blue incrusta from the dado to a cornice also of raw umber. There was matching chintz furniture that proved surprisingly comfortable; I sank into a chintz armchair and drank cognac from a snifter while H2 launched a ponderous story on the riveting subject of how he and Caro (who had at one time dated a Famous American Movie Star, I was informed) first met. The tale called for periodic bouts of sustained giggling from both H2 and Mrs H2. She wouldn't agree to go out with him, he insisted, she relented, he took her on an hours-long drive to a run-down chateau with no electricity and, apparently, ghosts. Caro called her husband Lord G, and when I asked why she called him that she answered *Why not?*, daring me with her deep-set brown eyes not to slit her belly open with the steak knife I had cached in the elastic waistband of my silk panties. Her intestines would slither out of the gash in her stomach like blood-soaked eels, dropping onto the polished cherrywood floor while she and her husband watched, helpless. She knows I'd do it. You have to admire courage in the face of a predator, or, failing that, me. Courage in the face of me is *something*.

Later H2 went to the piano, in the mysteries of which he was adept. Name a song and he could play it off the top of his head, with a short pause while he recollected the melody. 'Lean On Me', 'Life On Mars', 'Blank Space'. His voice was dreadful, and Caro's voice was if anything worse. I knew better than to join in singing. There's a sublime dissonance in the warbling of two off-key lovebirds. Adding a third voice, especially when it belongs not to a bird but a snake, ruins the effect.

24

In due course I was shown my room and left alone. When I pulled my laptop out of my rucksack, I realised I'd forgotten to ask for the Wi-Fi password. Worse, upon further investigation I found that my phone was missing. Had I left it somewhere? Or had it been confiscated? Either way, by accident or design, I was now wholly unable to communicate with *the outside world*. I put on my silk pyjamas and sneaked out of my room and back downstairs to look in the dark for my phone, feeling in the seat cushions of the chintz-covered couch I had been sitting on, checking on the various side tables and bookshelves I had passed or been sitting near. Mice are not quiet, but I was. When H2's voice spoke out of the darkness from the piano bench, I nearly jumped out of my second skin.

You will not find what you are looking for, he said.

What are you doing sitting in the dark? I asked.

I took your phone. I will provide a temporary replacement that will not have access to the internet.

That's extremely normal, I said.

Why are you vegan? This question has been keeping me awake. I sit at the piano when I cannot sleep.

You can't sleep because I'm a vegan?

Not *because* you are a vegan, but *why* you are a vegan.

I ate everything you served tonight, I said.

That means you are not a vegan because of ethical concerns. Also it means that you have no dietary problems with meat or dairy.

I can see why this would keep you awake.

Yes, he said.

That was sarcasm.

Yes, he said.

I'm a vegan, or I am when it's possible to be a vegan without causing anyone the slightest inconvenience, because I prefer vegetables and nuts to any other food. It's a question not of ethics or diet but of taste, I said.

Taste. That makes sense but at the same time it makes no sense. How can anyone not prefer the taste of butter to — what do you use in place of butter?

In cooking or in salads, olive oil. Which is also good with bread. Some good vegan cheeses have recently turned up in speciality shops.

Now you're mocking me, he said.

They're overpriced, but they exist. If you miss the taste of meat, which I never do, there are various types of tofu or seitan or other wheat proteins. But I eat vegetables, nuts and lots of fruit. Especially apples.

I do enjoy apples.

And I drink a lot, I said.

But naturally. Still, I don't understand how you developed these . . . tastes. You grew up in France, no?

Yes.

You perhaps had too much French food when you were a child? Too heavy for you?

Nothing like that. If I miss anything it's probably *boudin* — fresh *boudin*. And ham crêpes with Normandy cider.

Note to the reader: this conversation took place in French. I'm reconstructing it a little too verbatim from memory.

Then you are French after all, he said.

Did you doubt it?

It's my nature to doubt everything.

Good night, H2.

Good night, Van.

My first name on his tongue was a violation. If I were the sort of girl who took lots of showers, I would have taken a shower just to wash the shame away. I decided to take a shower anyway, because it had been a long and germy flight, and a shower or bath after an l. and g. f. can be restorative.

It was with the intention of taking a shower that I went to what I had been told was the guest bathroom, down the hall from the room where I was sleeping. The bathroom was appointed in black-and-white Métro tiles, a fashionable thing to do in bourgeois circles just then in *métropolitan* France, but I was dismayed to discover instead of a shower an enormous claw-footed bathtub. Without a showerhead of any kind, without a shower curtain of any kind: the idea being, one supposes, that if the master of the house were to happen accidentally to walk in on his guest taking a languorous bath in the claw-footed tub, nature would take its course and a clangorous tub fuck would ensue.

I was careful to lock the door and to wedge a chair under the knob as well. I had not calculated that upon approaching the tub and seizing the stopcocks that I would find the body of the eldest of H2's daughters, Temple, submerged in the water, naked except for long black gloves and a pair of stockings with garter belts embroidered with miniature percale roses. In her gloved hands she held a green apple out of which a tiny bite had been taken. She was clearly *in articulo mortis*, though for how long she'd been immersed I couldn't say. I'm not a medical examiner. When I turned round to leave the bathroom and rouse the household, I discovered the floor was covered in loose pearls. I slipped and fell, hard. After which I don't remember anything until I woke up in my bed the next morning.

This is another reason why I rarely bathe.

25

Thomas Early was the name of the boy I prized above all others. We met at a party in Los Angeles. I was there on business, to meet with the publisher of the *Los Angeles Review of Books*, who wanted to put me in charge of the section covering reviews of translations. I knew before I left the party that I would decline the offer, because there wasn't any money and the job sounded like a hassle. Writers and/or translators are a tendentious lot, but nothing compared to reviewers of writers and/or translators, who will cry havoc should you suggest that the translation of a novel written by a trans Icelandic woman whose translator was *not* a trans Icelandic woman need not be *a priori* worthless. I'm a hoot at parties.

The event was held at a house in Los Feliz on Nightingale Avenue (I remember the name of the street because I thought it quintessentially Los Angelesian) near Griffith Park. You could walk to the Observatory from there. Not me: I hate every species of physical exercise, and have no interest in whatever light-polluted view of the spotted globe one might obtain from that vantage point. Further: though I watch movies constantly, obsessively, I'm not the type of film fanatic who needs to visit the sites where her favourite (or often just famous) scenes were shot.

At that era Thomas lived in Los Angeles, pursuing a fruit-less career as a screenwriter after publishing two widely unread novels. He was a brilliant writer, but I've met a lot of brilliant writers. He may have been a genius, but I've no interest in genius. Genius can't tell me anything I don't already know, except perhaps exactly that: there are limits to what you can know, and you have reached them. Everything after that is speculation, or worse, faith.

Thomas had been asked to serve as Contributing Editor for the *LARB*, and had said yes, explaining that, unlike my post, his was decorative and required nothing from him but permission to use his name. *Whatever good that'll do them*, he said to me, as we huddled outside under a gas-powered heat lamp. It was November, and anytime the after-dark temperature in LA goes below seventy degrees Fahrenheit, heat lamps are deployed like glowing robot sentries across the cement patios and porches of Hollywood and its environs.

I had already decided that I would sleep with him that night, because he was tall and thin and had no dress sense and hair that went in every direction. I liked his boots, and later his books, and he talked about Godard and Fassbinder in ways that didn't make my skin crawl, which is difficult to do. He was just back from a six-week screenwriter's residency in Paris and had apparently studied French in school but he was shy using it, unless he was drunk, which made his French worse. I thought his heavy American accent cute.

I had accepted his offer to drink-drive me to my hotel when some knob from the Writer's Guild, which had funded his residency and apparently therefore considered him its property, cock-blocked me, so it was two months before I got to fuck him. Happily, it was my birthday when it happened. Best present ever.

26

After a few months, I convinced Thomas to relocate to New York and into my East Village apartment, which was big enough for five people, so obviously big enough for two. I taught him about jazz, he taught me about obscure British post-punk bands, and we went to galleries, museums and films. We ate a lot of prosciutto and unpasteurised French cheese. His favourite Singani cocktail was the Corpse Reviver #2 – which, as you will presently see, is keenly, morbidly ironic:

1 OZ SINGANI 63
1 OZ COINTREAU
1 OZ LEMON JUICE
1 DASH ABSINTHE
COCKTAIL CHERRY

STIR ALL INGREDIENTS OVER ICE, THEN
STRAIN INTO COUPE GLASS. GARNISH
WITH COCKTAIL CHERRY.

CORPSE REVIVER #2

SPONSORED CONTENT

It was my pleasure to make many of these cocktails for him. Thomas was borderline agoraphobic and I am not, but the life of a recluse suits me fine. His fear of going outside turned out to be justified. Going outside is what got him killed.

Here's how it happened.

One day three years into our blissful cohabitation I came home from shopping, already knackered and overwrought after battling the crowds (I lost, but it was close), and found him keen to skirmish over something he'd discovered nosing through my emails: specifically, evidence related to an ongoing Los Angeles-based affair I was having with a boy out there named Guy Forget, which, I know, sounds like a made-up name, and may well be made-up, but not by me.

I do not take kindly to people nosing through my emails. The affair was of no consequence, but it is no good telling a man who loves you that your other love affairs are of no consequence. For whatever reason (their friable egos), these affairs *matter* to them, and no amount of grovelling will convince them to put by their objurgation, which you will have to listen to at length, punctuated by heart-felt sobs. I have no time for any of this.

Take me as I am, Thomas, or do not take me at all, I told him, and the next time you are overcome by the itch to nose through my emails, I invite you instead to chop off your scrotum.

You can perhaps surmise that my attitude did not sit well with Thomas Early, but: he didn't get angry in the usual sense. He was not heated or irate. He was despondent, downcast, dejected, and that did not agree with my view of the proper way to respond to what I'd said. I expected my bitter words to be met with his bitter words, so that we could be said to have *exchanged words*, and things could take their usual shape from there, ending up with a night or part of a night spent by him on my Frank Gehry sofa or my cream-coloured fainting couch, apologies all around, and cathartic if inevitably disappointing make-up sex.

That is not what happened. Instead he sat on the ottoman opposite the fainting couch and slumped his shoulders: not crying, exactly – I do not allow crying in my apartment unless by me, at which time you may be invited to join me, though I have to go first – but his eyes were bright, which is a prelude to crying.

This quiet desperation in the face of my caged-lion rage only provoked a further leonine outburst, which again failed to stoke his fires, and I now thought him seriously damped for good, or for a good while. I could have, should have, left him alone and walked down to the street to fill my gut with a gallon of wine. I could have, should have, marched to my room and used my AK to engender an artificial eudemonic condition (more on this later, probably).

But I did not do either of these more judicious things. Instead I lost my temper so comprehensively that I insisted he vacate my apartment post-haste: I fairly shoved Thomas out of the door, by which I should clarify that I mean the door to my apartment, not the door to the lift to my apartment; because I have a floor to myself, there is a door between my apartment and the lift door. The reason I'm telling you this is that once the door to my apartment closed I did not wait to watch (though I could have, there's a window in the door) Thomas get into the lift, or see what button he pressed. He pressed the *up* button, which takes you up one *étage* to the actress Juno Temple's apartment, or what she uses as her apartment when she's in town. But Thomas didn't try to go into Juno Temple's apartment. He used the exit door at the end of the narrow hallway on her floor to take the stairs up to the roof. The door should have been locked. Loads of people told me in the following days that the door should have been locked.

Suicide strikes me as a failure of imagination. If you're disturbed enough to kill yourself, in my view, you've rather let the side down, and yourself as well. Death is obvious and undeniable: the scary clown at every happy birthday. I mean, I get it. There's no point to anything. But to me, *advocatus diaboli*, the pointlessness of everything is the best argument for anything. *Usefulness* is a fundamentally dishonest concept. Anything worth doing is as well worth *not* doing. Everything I do is nugatory, and that will always be the case. If I can help it.

When Thomas threw himself six storeys to the street below, I didn't notice. I heard the screech of car brakes and the blaring of car horns and the clamour of the street, but I did not attach any special importance to it. These were ordinary episodes on my street. On any street in New York. On any street in every city.

One further oddity, which proves or disproves the popular theory that I am a hypocrite. My apartment is the one from which Francesca Woodman jumped to her death. I'm fascinated by Francesca Woodman. Whereas I was disgusted by Thomas. Before he died. Now I'm just appalled.

27

Thomas Early's death was ruled a suicide, but it should have been ruled a murder, and I a murderer. I should have been locked away for life. Instead, I found myself alone in the early morning hours in a weirdly bright room with wallpaper patterned in blue upside-down triangles on a cadmium lemon background in a fugly house outside Paris waiting for a man who claims to be Not Michel Houellebecq to wake up, so that I can ask him whether his daughter Temple (if that's her name) is dead or alive, which is an awkward question first thing in the morning.

One makes the best of things when being kept in durance vile. I went down for coffee as soon as I heard anyone stir. The stirring person was the cook, or one of the cooks, or maybe she had multiple functions in the house, maybe she was H2's mistress or second wife or secretary or factotum. As long as she knew how to work the espresso machine I didn't care.

Her name was Virginie, and she did. The coffee was predictably not terrible, but not great either. I mean, we weren't in Italy, where even truck stop coffee has been blessed by the gods. I heard a wild inburst of childish laughter and multiple footsteps hurtling through the corridors above, which set my mind at ease on the subject of dead Temple versus live Temple, and fearing an encounter with one of these attenuated hominids I quickly absented myself to the furthest room from the kitchen I could find, which turned out to have a side door leading by a gravel path overgrown with hyssop and gorse to a garden I had not seen/had not been shown when I arrived the previous evening. I took my coffee and sat on a low stone bench under a chestnut tree in need of pruning. Clustered in a nearby copper beech, doves cooed softly as I sipped my double espresso. Two Procilla Beauties flitted by, and a Violet-Spotted Charax. The garden had an unkempt and unloved grandeur that I found acutely reposeful. Don't know how long or little I'd slept but I didn't feel at all tired. On the contrary, my brain buzzed with ideas, like the ruby-throated *colibri* tracing discrete parallelograms round the wild rose bush next to the bench.

The sound of footsteps on the gravel path startled me. I turned to see H2 approaching.

You are enjoying yourself, he said.

I must have had a dumb smile on my face. He was enjoying my heartbeat of happiness while at the same time ruining it. A special talent.

Good morning, I said. The coffee made me sound like a lynx gargling in a dark cave.

We are running late. You have had enough coffee? You would like something to eat perhaps?

The coffee's enough for me, I said. Not much of a breakfast person.

I sound like an asshole in French. To be fair, everyone sounds like an asshole in French.

28

H2 wanted to go to his summer house in Cap Ferret. He said we'd be more comfortable there, more isolated, better able to work. He'd have his private cook and his housekeeper, but we wouldn't see them, and the kids and the wife were to visit only on weekends, at which point I would move into a nearby seaside hotel, mostly empty at this time of the year; which if I have not mentioned yet was November. I was sold the instant he pointed out that I wouldn't have to see his kids again, but choice wasn't really on the menu, me-wise, at this juncture.

The summer house was smaller than the Paris house, but it was right on the water; so that it might more properly be called a rickety sea prison. It led to a short pier where H2 docked his boat, which was *plus grand* than what I'd call a boat but *plus petit* than what you'd call a yacht. It was a sailboat of some twenty metres in length, and H2 claimed to be an expert sailor. He'd piloted his boat down the Atlantic coast through the straits of Gibraltar all round the Mediterranean as far as Turkey.

I'm not a boat person. That much should be obvious from my lack of precision when ventilating the subject of H2's sailboat. It might not have been a sailboat. It might have been a sloop, a cutter, a ketch, a yawl, a schooner, a gaffer or a barque in a complicated metaphor about the unalterable nature of love. It might have been a dinghy. Nor could I discuss its rigging, its tack, its clew, its jib (or the cut of same), its boom, its roach, its luff, its leach or its halyard(s). This is fascinating stuff, *sans doute*, if you've a nautical bent. I've not.

But I don't mind looking at the ocean. In particular the rugged Atlantic coastline near Cap Ferret, which though different in latitude reminds me of the coastline at Kennebunkport in Maine and at Lowestoft in East Anglia. Not for me tropical climes with pure white sand and placid aquamarine waters. Not for me palm trees, daiquiris and carcinogenic ozone holes. Not for me acres of bronzed flesh caked with powdered coral or the dung of horseshoe crabs splayed on technicolour polyester beach towels smeared with suntan lotion and semen. The beach is a place where a man can feel. How does the rest go? It doesn't matter. That's my experience of the beach – men feeling me, either literally, or with ravenous eyes.

I don't like the beach. That's clear. But I don't mind the shore, especially where it's rocky and untraversable. I am littoral-minded.

We had taken the TGV to Bordeaux, where a car had picked us up and driven us to Cap Ferret. We arrived in the afternoon, but it was so foggy and dark it might as well have been evening. November is my favourite time of year in any part of any country north of the equator. I'll take the whole of November through February, when the nights are long and the days have hardly stretched their limbs and blinked open their sleepy eyes before twilight dims to a crepuscular flush, suffusing the landscape with violet and blue, glinting off the (ideally) rain-macerated streets, shading the green bronzes (dripping or snow-hatted or bare in the gelid air). Couldn't see or hear much of the rickety sea prison's exterior on arrival: the pilings of the pier disappearing into the fret, the silhouette of the boat, its surfy rasp.

The apartment in the East Village has colossal floor-to-ceiling windows facing the street, so when I heard the commotion I could easily have gotten up and walked over to the window, looked down and seen Thomas lying face down on the ground, vivid cerise blood pooling round his crushed head. But I didn't.

29

I don't suppose you think I'm being too hard on myself?
No, more likely you think that by condemning myself I'm
letting myself off, in the way that someone tells you *I'm a
cunt* and that's supposed to absolve them of being a cunt.
Self-awareness is no excuse. Still and all, I don't have the
requisite decadence for self-pity.

Where are my manners? Let me refresh your drink, Juno.
Why not try a Moscow Mule?

1.5 OZ SINGANI 63
.5 OZ. LIME JUICE
1 BAR SPOON COMBIER CRÈME DE
PAMPLEMOUSSE ROSE
2 OZ GINGER BEER
CANDIED GINGER
SPRIG OF MINT

MOSCOW MULE

SHAKE FIRST THREE INGREDIENTS WITH
ICE THEN STRAIN INTO COPPER MUG WITH
ICE. TOP WITH GINGER BEER AND GARNISH
WITH CANDIED GINGER AND MINT.

Thomas Early is dead by my inductile hand and heart. Had
I shown any empathy for the boy I adored, he'd probably be
alive. So I guess I'm a cunt?

By the time we got to H2's summer house I was half-drunk. I had stashed a bottle of Singani 63 from duty-free in my rucksack, and housed it on the TGV in the toilet. That probably sounds grosser than it was. The toilets on the TGV are spacious and sometimes clean, and when you're a girl, people don't give you much shit about taking a lot of time. Within reason. After ignoring three or four people coming up, pressing the button to open the automatic door and, on seeing that the toilet was occupied, banging on the plastic door hard enough to rattle the walls (this is easy to do – the walls are not well built), I finally decided I'd had enough Singani, though I still took my sweet time washing my hands. When I exited, I shrugged at the peevish business dudes who'd been waiting for ten minutes and said, *Just got my period.*

As happens so often in what we call real life, I *had* just gotten my period. Thus the alcohol was not merely a palliative for my hangover but for the clawing pain in my womb. I took a handful of ibuprofen because a nurse once told me that you could take 800 mg of ibuprofen without any risk to your liver. *As long as you don't drink too much.* Smiley face emoticon.

Once we arrived at the mist-mantled beach house H2 was preoccupied and didn't say much. He went from room to room while I stood like a traveller from an antique land in the hallway. I once watched a documentary depicting the fussy mating ritual of a particoloured tropical bird who, before puffing his feathers and performing an elaborate dance, scrupulously cleans the forest floor of debris, the better to impress his prospective mate. No idea why that should hop to mind just then.

H2 showed me to my room and I dropped my rucksack in a chair by the door.

In about an hour I should think Morgan will have something ready for dinner, he said.

See you in an hour, I said, and shut the door in his face.

I'm a cunt, by the by.

Here's a picture of the view from my window:

30

Things didn't improve at dinner. By things I mean my attitude, and by dinner I mean the feast of shellfish and fresh vegetables that Morgan the cook prepared for us. H2 insisted on opening what he said was an extraordinary Sauternes, and I allowed his insistence to overrule my inclination against insistence. My period gives me headaches which I would call migraines except they're not technically migraines, they just hurt like a motherfucker. Mother*fucker*. The audio version of this book is going to be a blast to record. Note to person narrating the audiobook: fuck you. But say it like you're mad at yourself. Fuck you. Now say it like you're mad at me. Fuck *you*. This has got to be more fun than whatever else you're getting paid to read out loud.

This isn't going to work for me, I said to H2 as I slid a garlicked and buttered mussel down my throat.

What do you mean? he said.

Staying in this house. I'll come over during the day but I require solitude at night. Otherwise I'll have trouble sleeping, and then I'll have trouble working.

Perhaps you have the *décalage horaire*, he said.

I don't get jet lag. I travel loads, same as you. My body's used to it. I just don't do well in other people's houses.

I had in mind the vision of his dead daughter in the bath-tub but figured I'd save myself the trouble of depicting said vision.

Put me up in the hotel where you're planning to put me up on weekends anyway, and we'll take it from there, yeah?

I don't see what difference it makes, but if that is what you wish, we will arrange it.

That is what I wish.

We will arrange it.

Thank you, I said. This Sauternes isn't bad.

I thought you might like it. I also have an excellent pear brandy that we should try.

I'm all for pear brandy, I said. I'm pro-brandy full stop. Singani is a type of brandy, in that it's distilled from muscat grapes. If brandy were a political party I would probably vote.

I prefer champagne to any other drink, he said.

You can't possibly mean that.

Why not? he asked.

Champagne is for amateurs and tourists. I'm not voting for anyone who drinks champagne.

I'm not running for office.

Lucky for you, because you just lost my vote.

Are you finished with the mussels?

Yes. (I wasn't.)

Shall we take the brandy out on the terrace?

Of course you have a terrace.

We went and sat out on his terrace, which had a view of the sea, except it was too dark to see the sea. But you could hear the sea. You could smell the sea. You could feel the salt spray stinging your face. This was imaginary salt spray, conjured by your sense of touch, by your senses of hearing and smell, respectively, but you know the drill

As well you should.

I'm not OK. I can't keep fronting. I cannot front.

The wind picked up. I thought I heard in the combination of wind and night rote the sound of city traffic and people screaming, though, you know, that was probably impossible.

31

On the terrace he produced a retro Motorola RAZR and a high-tech key the size of a credit card for my hotel room. He put the phone on the table at which we were sitting and slid it across the metal grille of the tabletop. It's hard to slide things across a tabletop with a metal grille. The rectilinear mesh of the grille, especially when painted, as this was (matt black), causes friction that will radically impede any non-spherical object unless you use a deal of force. The problem with using a deal of force is that the object will more often than not fly across the tabletop and over the edge, onto the paving stones of the terrace, and (in the case of a cheaply made flip phone) break apart. Luckily for H2, I have feline reflexes and caught the phone just as it fell over the edge of the table but before it reached the ground.

As discussed, he said.

I flipped it open and scrolled through the contacts. There were three. My parents, my sister and H2.

If I try to call a number that's not in the contacts?

You will be unable to do so. Parental controls permit wide latitude in restricting outgoing calls.

You're treating me like a child.

Not at all. My children can call whomever they like.

I took a sip of pear brandy.

Why is my sister's number in here? We never talk.

He said the usual romantic thing about twins: that unbreakable bond; an almost extrasensory connection.

Not us, I said. We accrued none of the benefits sometimes mooted as compensatory for sharing space in one's mother's womb. Even less so now; we inhabit different worlds. I'm not even sure this is her current number. She has to change numbers every week to avoid stalkers and fans and me.

You know she has a a big premiere in Paris for her new film next month?

No, I do not know she has a a big premiere in Paris for her new film next month. I've never been to any of her premieres.

Not even for the James Bond movie?

Especially not the James Bond movie. Which I have moreover not seen.

I find this attitude puzzling, he said.

'Tis pity she's a whore.

He looked at the sea instead of me and took out a packet of American Spirit Yellows. Offered one to me. I declined, and he lit up with a cheap plastic Bic, which he placed next to the pack on the table. Exhaled sharply.

Tomorrow we will start working, he said. The idea of the book is ambitious. I want to retell the history of Western civilisation from the point of view of a dove who has become immortal by eating a seed soaked in the blood of Christ.

Blood of Christ, I intoned, not believing him. Sipped the brandy. Which really was excellent.

32

I decamped to the hotel after dinner. Because it was the off season and the hotel was gigantic, I felt as though I were the only one staying there, and I'm certain the skeletal off-season staff resented that their off-seasonal rest had been disrupted by a gorgeous stranger (I put in the part about me being gorgeous to remind myself, and you). I got some unfriendly stares from the female staff, and some ambiguous stares from the males, but I ignored everyone and deadbolted myself into my first-floor room, which was unexpectedly large and full of shadows. I tried to drink myself to sleep with the rest of the bottle of pear brandy H2 had gifted me. Didn't work. I lay unmoving in my bed in the dark for a solid semi-hour, gazing at the adumbral patterns moving across my ceiling, occasionally swigging straight from the bottle; then got up and turned on the light at the desk and opened my laptop. There was no wireless connection. I wasn't surprised.

I closed the laptop and went outside for a walk. The seafront was deserted, and many of the surrounding buildings – also hotels – were latent, some run down to near-ruin. Walking up a side street towards the town, I found a woman's left shoe with a broken heel. I picked it up; it was fairly new, except for the heel, and comely. The leather was supple, dyed a delicate blueish green and decorated with a large cabochon, triangular in shape and metallic gold in colour. On looking closer, I saw there was on the right side of the pointed tip a spot of what could have been dried blood but which was probably dirt.

I put the shoe back where I had found it, on the uneven paving stones of the side street next to a granite staircase. Looking up the steps of the staircase I saw a heavy door painted black, with no handle or lock or intercom or doorbell that I could see. Stepping back, I could see that the house was between numbers nine and eleven on the odd side of the street, but had no number itself. In the place where you'd expect to see a house number, there was instead an eye carved into the stone the wrong way up, enclosed in an upside-down equilateral triangle. I continued up the little street until I found myself at a café – Café Rudolph, on the south-west corner of Place de l'Opéra – that appeared to be open.

There were two other customers in Café Rudolph, both sitting at the bar, and I slid into a booth near the windows to avoid having to talk to either of them. I ordered a small coffee from the ungarrulous waiter and thanked the sidereal entities once again for making French waiters by law surly and speechless. My coffee arrived presently, and it wasn't, tbh, any good, but with the supplement of a lump of Perruche, it didn't need to be. I looked out on the square.

A tow-headed girl in a tattered light blue dress was selling flowers on the opposite side of the street. I thought this odd for two reasons: 1) Who sells flowers in the street at midnight in this empty town? and 2) The girl looked like Temple, H2's daughter, whom I'd seen dead in a bathtub only a night or was it a thousand and one nights before.

Things I am learning: whether you like it or not, stories happen; all the time, even while you're sipping bad espresso in a coastal café minding your own beeswax; they are busy breeding in the dark; developing minds and even bodies of their own; bleeding into one another, careless of the carpet or the cobblestoned street; leaving their spoor for others to follow.

I will follow.

33

When I woke in my hotel room bed, which was both too big for me and smaller than I'm accustomed to, I spent several minutes examining my room in more detail than I had the night before. The ceiling was of some interest, painted sky blue with a large red phoenix in flight towards the left-hand corner as observed from the bed, which faced the street. Surrounding the phoenix was a cortège of butterflies rendered with unusually accurate detail. I could identify an Acadian Hairstreak, several Monarchs, a Clouded Yellow, an Arctic Fritillary and a cloud of Cabbage Whites. Why these butterflies should be accompanying a phoenix and where they might be headed was left to the imagination; I decided they were on a mission to alert Nancy Wake (the White Mouse) in the Forest of Tronçais of the approach of German forces.

I went to the windows, which were large, the panes of glass similarly large, and heavy. I didn't try to open them. I looked down at the street, which was as empty now as it had been on my return to the hotel around two in the morning.

Here is a picture of a photograph of two swans and their young:

A gang of ruffians ran by, followed shortly by another gang of ruffians pelting the first gang of ruffians with stones and bottles. None of the kids looked to be older than thirteen or fourteen, but I'm not good at guessing ages, so let's call the age range of the ruffians (who were certainly not the same age, judging by their relative sizes) somewhere between nine and fourteen. I use the term ruffians because it seems appropriate – they were dressed shabbily, had wild hair, and their faces were smeared with dirt; or they hadn't washed in months, which, as you know, I applaud, but there are limits. One has to establish limits or liminal zones in which to operate or one will never get anywhere.

These gangs of ruffians would never get anywhere. They were doomed by systemic failures on a scale that I had trouble conceptualising, because it hadn't failed only them, it had failed everyone, for generations, and will spell doom for humanity, sooner rather than later. Those failures and that doom are tied in partly with end-stage capitalism and partly with the damage inflicted by end-stage capitalism on the environment, which, I mean, look out the window. Not the window in my hotel in Cap Ferret, which is apparently overrun by gangs of unruly children, but the window in wherever you are, whenever you are. The evidence is in front of your eyes. Perhaps you can't see it but it's there. *Ad oculos*, as the kids would say had they studied Latin.

Latin predates the language of the Angles and the Saxons, and thus the first forms of primitive Anglo-Saxon were intermingled with Latin influences. Cruel is an interesting example. Derived originally from *crudus*, meaning rough or raw, it has evolved in mostly logical ways from that rough/raw material to its present adjectival use in the sense of 'wilfully causing pain or suffering'. But wait, there's more! For reasons I don't pretend to grasp, cruel can be a verb in informal Australian English. *She cruelled his chances.*

Given the opportunity, I will cruel your chances. I don't mean anything by it. I'm not a nice person, and if I see a chance to do mischief, I will nine times out of ten take that chance. The other time out of ten I may judge the chance not worth the bother. That's you being lucky. That's you being lucky and not knowing or appreciating it. In other words, that's you every day of your life. Luck has no Latin root. Nor does life. Make of that what you will.

I am a centuried relic from a distant shrine. That much I can tell you, but the rest you'll have to discover without my help.

34

I quickly dressed and went back over to H2's summer house for coffee. Now that I was sober, I wanted to hear more about the insane idea for his novel. Once again, I was disappointed.

Regarding this supposed immortal pigeon of yours, I said.

I don't want to talk any more about it, H2 said. I shouldn't have mentioned anything.

But how—

That is the part of the process in which I am most interested, he said. How. How can you translate a book that has not yet been written? Or before it has been written. By telling you the general idea, I have, I fear, already impeded the process. Please don't ask me anything else.

Fine by me.

I shrugged, already falling back into Gallic habits, shrugging when presented with the slightest obstacle. I tore a piece of bread from the baguette on the kitchen table. The table was covered in a blue-and-white checked oilcloth that had not been wiped down since breakfast, judging from the blear lemniscate of coffee rings near the basket of baguettes.

Did you know that the Sanskrit word *anus* can be translated as 'atom' in the latter's classical Greek sense of 'uncut' or 'indivisible'? H2 said.

Yup, I said, my mouth full of baguette. I chewed and swallowed. The question is, how do you know that?

I read it in a book. It's interesting. Perhaps you know it, a biography of—

I held up my hand to stop him.

I don't care. The biography of I Don't Care is a firm fave in my house.

You're out of sorts this morning.

You're an *anus*.

Thank you.

The ungentle sun pouring through both open windows enveloped the kitchen in a citrusy gauze through which I was having trouble seeing. I put on sunglasses.

I had trouble sleeping last night, so I went to a café.

Ah. Café Maximilian, no doubt?

No, Café Rudolph. On the south-west corner of Place de l'Opéra.

I don't know this place. Café Maximilian is excellent. I am good friends with the owner.

This place was fine. On my way there, I saw an unusual house. It was on a little side street called Rue Mouchette. It didn't have a street number, but it was between numbers 9 and 11.

Then it was 9 bis.

You'd think, but, as I said, there was no number. There was however an insignia carved in stone next to the door. An upside-down eye in an upside-down triangle.

That *is* curious, he said.

No chance you've noticed it?

I don't spend time exploring. I'm too busy.

Did you remember to get me the Rhodia notebooks I asked for? I had not asked H2 to get me any notebooks. I was toying with him.

Did you ask for that? I'm sorry. My memory has been letting me down lately. I forget the simplest things.

I hear prickly ash is good for that.

Good for the memory?

No. I just like saying the words *prickly ash*.

Tell me, he said.

He leaned closer, his halcyon smile disguising, no doubt, baleful intent.

Have you made much progress?

You mean have I made much progress on the translation?

Yes. He was eager to know. I was as eager to disappoint him.

Naturally, he replied, swallowing his disappointment. You've barely had time to settle in, he said. You understand I'm excited.

I do. But if we're not going to discuss the plot, we're going to have to cover some basic principles in order for me to proceed.

Of course.

Basic principle one: stop asking me how I'm progressing. It checks rather than spurs me. Basic principle two: I will show you what I've done when I'm ready to show you what I've done. That said, I will show you pages as I go, both as a gesture of good faith and so that I don't go too far in a particular direction without your oversight. Basic principle three: while your input at any stage is welcome, I alone will make the primary creative decisions as I go, and I will decide when my work is finished.

That is acceptable to me.

Good. This way we'll avoid wasting time. Some people believe no time is wasted, ever; but I don't hold those people in high esteem.

I'm inclined to agree with you.

Though there's something to be said for a way of looking at things that discounts past, present and future, and concentrates on the between points. Have you read the *Bardo thos grol*?

I don't think so.

More commonly known as the *Tibetan Book of the Dead*, though that's a misleading and incorrect translation.

I've heard of the *Book of the Dead*, but I've never read it. Hippy nonsense.

Yeah, well, it's not.

I would not care to argue the point.

It's a foundational text of human civilisation. But, OK, even I've never read it in the original, because I could never be arsed with the Tibetan-Burmese languages. An exact translation of the title would be something like *Liberation through Understanding the Between*, I'm told. That's an ungainly, rough rendering. The Tibetans believed in a panoply of between-states of existence, but the one I'm interested in is that between present and future, or between past and present. In other words the instant right now, which is never right now because as soon as it happens it's gone. The instant between instances is where the action is, but there's no time for action. It's where thought resides, but there's no time for thought. It's the *what* of all decisions but those decisions have been predetermined by the past, or some version of the past. Do you know much about decision trees? They're an integral part of machine learning, which scares some people, but in my opinion the sooner machines take over the better.

H2 thought that over. Or was at a loss for words. Or was giving me a moment to collect myself.

Would you like some more coffee? he asked after a while.

35

I drink too much coffee.

How much is too much? I suppose if you asked Balzac he would answer *more than fifty cups a day*, since he had a history of health problems, some of them no doubt related to drinking too much coffee, and anyway he died at fifty-one. If you asked an ordinary American person your answer would be *no such thing*. But American persons have no idea how coffee is supposed to taste or how to make it or what it is. Many independently run shops, usually found in college towns, and one or two minor chains can make decent coffee, but the percentage of the American population that knows of these independent shops is tiny, and the percentage that patronises Starbucks and down is vast (Starbucks being terrible, anything below Starbucks being worse and worse and worse until you arrive by a conterminous vector of degradation at Denny's). So fuck American persons and their opinions.

The medical profession is divided on the subject of too much coffee, or on appropriate dosages of caffeine and its associated health benefits and risks. Studies have been conducted. Conclusions have been reached. Scholarly papers have been peer-reviewed and vetted and printed in academic journals, then misquoted, mischaracterised, taken out of context, sensationalised, shortened and squeezed into clickbait. But yes, I drink too much coffee. Not by Balzac's standards but by any reasonable person's standards. I defy you to find a reasonable person. At least in America. It's not possible. See: the news, all the time, every day and night and day (the distinction between night and day, Cole Porter's efforts notwithstanding, has always been a little unclear to me, possibly because I drink so much coffee). The news is a mirror — not many American persons know this, having been brought up to believe a mirror is a mirror, but that's just fustian and fantasy.

What should concern you is the amount of Provigil I take. Especially when combined with my above-average coffee intake. Provigil isn't a stimulant per se, but it has stimulating effects. I used to know more about the specific *sequelae* but when I looked more closely into the way Provigil (or moda-finil, to give it its generic name) works on brain chemistry, I freaked out and had to take three Klonopin to calm down enough to forget I had investigated the *sequelae* of Provigil (modafinil) on brain chemistry.

Not to say that I didn't still accept H2's offer of more coffee and chug it down.

If you don't mind, I'd like to go back to the hotel and start working, I said.

That's fine. I'm leaving in a few minutes. I have to go back to Paris for a few days. I do have a chemical company to run, you know.

The prospect of H2 leaving for a few days was immensely appealing to me. I think he could tell by looking at my face, which must have lightened like the sun reappearing from an umbrageous cloud.

Not that I don't trust you, he said, but my associates have instructions to keep you from leaving the immediate area of the hotel or this house. You may feel free to come and go as you wish.

But only to or near those two places.

Anything you need or want will be brought to you. Help yourself to my library. And Morgan will be on hand whenever you want him to cook for you.

I'm fine with the hotel food, I said.

Suit yourself. Morgan will be here either way.

OK.

I wish you good luck with your work.

OK.

You raised your hand! I wasn't sure you were still listening. Just because you were lying down on the couch with your eyes closed, and occasionally snoring, I jumped to the conclusion that . . . Immaterial. My mistake. You have a question, Juno?

You think so? Too much reflexive dialogue? You mean like when I write down every time I say 'OK' or 'Sure' or 'Huh' or 'Go fuck yourself, Juno Temple, what the hell do you know about writing a book anyway?' Kidding! I so appreciate your constructive criticism, neighbour. I mean that sincerely, as the trench-coated drummer from U2 once said to me at a party for Patti Smith's photography hosted by Michael Stipe (please contact the Help Desk for a fuller explanation of these gnomic pop culture references). I knew Drummy didn't mean that sincerely, because if you have to say you mean something sincerely, you obviously don't mean that sincerely.

But unlike him, I do mean that sincerely.

36

For the next few days I rarely left my hotel room, working fitfully and without accomplishing much. There was neither a *Petit* nor a *Grand Larousse*, much less a *Webster's Third International*, in H2's puny seaside library. I didn't mind the lack of online, but I did miss the books. I like to begin as a Luddite and progress towards progress. I start off long-hand, pencil on paper, before committing to the screen of my laptop. The work feels more tactile and therefore rewarding when you do it by hand, and it's such a pain to revise that you tend to write more carefully. Or I do.

Research is more cumbersome when you're forced back on the Big Books of Reference, but these have the advantage of being reliable, or anyway difficult to disprove. Eventually I will submit the text to the infra dig of spell check and online glossaries and dictionaries, because my aim is accuracy not purity, but if, like me, you're smitten with words themselves – their sounds, textures, associations, histories, connections, on and on to the break of dawn – then you will retain, as I do, a reverence for the twenty-volume *OED* that other, better souls reserve for sacred writings.

Who the hell am I kidding. I retain a reverence? For a fucking dictionary? Look, I do love words, that should be obvious by now, but what I love even better is showing off, which is why I will always pick the obscure or antiquated or even just flat out wrong word whenever possible if I think there's a shot it'll make me sound smarter than I am. Which is already pretty goddamn smart. But it's never enough, is it? That stupid cliché (as opposed to all the smart clichés) about how you can never be too rich or too thin – for me, yes, that, but also you can never be too smart or too hot or too, I don't know, just *superior*. Without my superiority to everyone else on earth who am I, really? Just a privileged, entitled, trust fund bitch who killed her lover. A murderess, an adulteress, a whore, a cassowary (flightless bird), a logothete, a hopeless toper, a volatile demirep. Sounds irresistible, I know. Well, boys and girls and non-binary hotties, the good news is that I am newly available! All of this and more (terms to be determined) can be yours for only three easy payments of your life force, made out to V. Salomon c/o Lucifer, the Original Poser. (Surely you don't need our address.)

It's time for me to admit that my plan to translate H2's book before it's been written has no hope of succeeding, and never did. What I initially had in mind was a kind of extension of Osvaldo Lamborghini's 'first publish, then write' gambit, except on a broader scale. What upon further reflection I developed as The Way was an extension of the idea that 'all writing is a form of translating', which now that I put it down in words sounds sophomoric; but there's a germ of the real in its truistic heart. The problem is, what I now realise I had in mind is translating (writing) my own book (book) and not H2's unwritten opus, or anyone else's for that matter.

For the punters in the back: this book is that book.

Now I just have to figure out a way to let H2 down softly.

I admire English because of its long battle with French and Latin after the Norman Conquest. Though not unscathed, the language endured, thanks to a thousand anonymous bards, thanks to John Wycliffe and John Gower and other people often named John. John Lydgate, one of the first English poets to wear spectacles, was a monk in the Benedictine abbey at Bury St Edmunds in Suffolk around 1385 CE. He was commissioned by Henry V to translate Giovanni delle Colonne's thirty-thousand-line *Historia Troiana*, which took eight years. He also translated Boccaccio's thirty-six-thousand-line *De casibus illustrium virorum*, among other things, and found time to write his own *Siege of Thebes*, which pretends to be a lost Canterbury tale. In the fourteenth century English had more dialects than literates. The North couldn't understand the South, the Middle could understand a little of both, and the East and the West, because closer to the coasts, understood most and a lot else, too. In the end the South won, because the South was London, and London became the world, for better and for much, much worse.

French has been less changeable over the centuries, insofar As She Is Written. I say nothing of the giddy-making varieties of patois that existed from village to village across the country well into the twentieth century, nor of the *langue d'oc* that prevailed in the South and traces of which can still be found in Provence and as far off as Spain and Italy. Old French was indexed by the ninth century, and the establishment of the Académie Française in 1635 means that a native

French speaker today can read without difficulty the essays of Montaigne (with modernised spelling), a rough contemporary of Shakespeare, more easily than a native English speaker can read Shakespeare. Early medieval *chansons de geste* are a cinch in the original Old French compared with Chaucer, whose fourteenth-century Middle English is incomprehensible without a tour guide. To me. Which is to say, I believe this to be the case. *Credibile est, quia ineptum est. Certum est, quia impossibile.*

A clouded, greenish mirror was tacked up on the wall above my desk in my hotel room, cracked, roughly trapezoidal in shape, bounded at the top by two right angles with ground edges and by a slightly curved oblique line with a sharp edge forming the bottom. I ran the tips of my fingers over the features of my face in the mirror; the mirror distorted at the point where it was cracked in a short, straight, vertical line the length of my face from forehead to chin. I could feel no crack in my face itself, but that doesn't mean it wasn't there.

There are, as I said, limits to everything, even those things that are by definition without limits, such as the void. One withal expects a limit, though I have not yet found it, to my belief in the void: in nothingness as the central fact of existence, before or behind which all other facts stand in serried ranks of insignificance. The apocalypse, or revelation if you prefer the Latin-derived option, is the realisation that there is no ego, no *I am*, no *Great I Am*. Where we go from here depends on you, as that fellow says in that thing.

37

A book, or at least this book, that is to say *my* book, is an invitation to enter into the reader's own spiritual life. The greatest book ever written (jury's still out, not expected to return any time this millennium) is to my eyes at least a finger, pointing: Look! You follow the finger, you look, and you see, but whether you see what the writer intends, or something utterly different, is an outcome not just of the writer's genius but of yours. In that sense every book is a choose-your-own-adventure.

In another sense, a book is never finished. Nor a poem, a song, a painting, a building, a person. Nothing has been or will ever be complete. Everything is in the process either of becoming or unbecoming, and it is the task of the artist not to make something new but to make something present.

Assuming the present exists. Quantum theory bulks large in mathematics, physics and comic book movies nowadays; I find most quantum-derived speculation endlessly interesting, if ultimately pointless (this is a joke about superposition), but most of this, including quantum computing, and ideas about the singularity – the day when machines achieve self-consciousness, or when artificial intelligence becomes self-aware, however you want to put it – ignores what I consider the most important bit or byte. A quantum world is still, at root, a digital world. And a digital world is a binary world. In a binary world there are only 1s and 0s. Even if the 1 can be where the 0 is or in two places at the same time or not anywhere, we're still only talking about binaries, and I wonder why no one talks about the spaces between the 1 and the 0. If you look at any random binary sequence – 01100110 01110101 01100011 01101011 00100000 01101111 01100110 01100110, for example – there are spaces between the 1 and the 0. No matter what type size or font you use, there will always be a space between any given 1 and any given 0 and its proximate digit. That space is irreducible. The shapes themselves dictate the space. Give something shape, even theoretical or imaginary shape, and it will require space. And that space is where everything that happens happens. It's not about time. There is no time. It's about space. There is no space.

If whatever this is, this chronicle of events, this live blog of my live journal of my weird world holiday, this travelogue, mystery novel, recipe file, notes for something else, commonplace book, diary, grocery list, exegesis, eisegesis, apologue, selvedge or helve, prolonged annotation, coping, oriel, croft, pillion, rushlight, unction, translation, if this *thing* sees natural or artificial light, it will be about the spaces between the binary code of our existence. There would otherwise be no point in my writing any of this down, nor would there be any point in your reading it. If I achieve what I have set out to do, not just the point of my book but the book itself will only ever exist in the between space. The between is maybe where you'll be able to find H2's book, if you're interested. I admit that I no longer am. The between is where all books come from. It's where everything comes from. It's the umbilicus of every good goddamn *res* in the universe. It's the brief crack of light before the void. Blink and you'll miss it.

You blinked.

38

Everyone's looking for transcendence, but no one wants to put in the work. We want shortcuts to the way out, or failing that a map. Not a faulty compass and a mordant good luck bellowed after us as we start hiking in the wrong direction at the wrong time, with insufficient supplies and uncomfortable shoes. But we'll never get more than that because the exits have been deliberately hidden, and in some cases may no longer exist.

A system of thought must always have an architectonic connection or coherence, that is, a connection in which one part always supports the other, though the latter does not support the former, in which ultimately the foundation supports all the rest without being supported by it, and the apex is supported without supporting. On the other hand, a single thought, however comprehensive, must preserve the most perfect unity. A book with a beginning and an end must *a priori* fail to achieve the necessary coherence to support either an epistemology or a unity of thought.

Because this book will have a beginning and an end, in order for it to succeed the reader will have had to read every preceding book and every subsequent book.

No one expects you to do that, not even me. Not sure it's possible, though in my twenty-nine years I've made an effort. By the time I'm done, if, despite indications to the contrary, I'm gifted a normal Western woman's lifespan on this granite planet, I'll have stared at more than my share of signs and symbols impressed on dead trees and dumb screens. But as any major Buddha will tell you, the difference between the wisdom of experience and the wisdom of learning is chasmic; you could say I'm working on the former at the expense of the latter.

And so this whatever-it-is I'm writing is by definition destined to fail. I'm OK with that. *The Failure* might be a good title, though I'm sure some tosser's already used it. If I had to choose a title right now, it would be *The Illusion of Consent*. For what I expect are obvious reasons. Maybe too-obvious, in which case it wouldn't be a good title, but I never said it was a good title. It's the title I would pick if forced to make a choice. The fact that I might be forced to make a choice illustrates the title. Well, there's that.

Has anyone told you that you have beautiful eyes? Though you probably don't. The number of people with beautiful eyes on the planet is fewer than ten at any given time. This is a fact easily demonstrable by applying any of the six or seven senses available during samadhi to the world's population, and provable in a court of law. I happen to be one of the handful who have verifiably beautiful eyes, and believe me, it is no big deal. You get tired of hearing it from everyone you meet, because it's the first thing they notice, and for some reason people blurt out the first thing they notice when you meet them.

You have beautiful eyes, the story goes.
Thank you, it continues.
A wisp of silence.
Would you— it continues.
No. The story ends.

39

When H2 left, and I was alone in the hotel, I thought about legging it, sure. I didn't see what anyone could do to stop me. He told me he had people keeping an eye on me – the whole hotel could be on his payroll – but I didn't see how anyone could prevent me from walking however far to the train station *guichet* and zip-lining to a distant town. I could have gone anywhere. Not just back to NYC, which would be the first place H2 would come looking, but anywhere. A train to Barcelona or Geneva or Berlin or Milan would not be expensive, and if I paid cash for the ticket I would be hard to track. Not impossible, but hard.

I didn't leave. Once, though, I did venture outside, to the *terrasse* of the adjacent Café Maximilian, facing the beach. I sat down mechanically on a metal folding chair with chipped and rusting slats, like me abandoned in this out-of-season landscape: an ancient city after the flood of burning ash, a village square the morning after the air raid, a seaside resort half-destroyed by equinoctial storms.

Reaching into my rucksack, I pulled out a pile of folders and set them before me, brushing away flakes of dull, pale green paint that, where they had come away, had left reddish-brown constellations on the disc of sheet metal that formed the top of the table on which my left elbow had come to rest. I raised my eyes. The two policemen were there, in civilian clothes but clearly recognisable. Light-coloured raincoats belted with casual haste. Rain-slicked shoes. I had the impression that this scene had transpired at least once before.

'In these schemes, the mind-body complex begins at birth and ceases at death, except for mental consciousness, which changes for the between-being since it is no longer embedded in matter and preoccupied with the evidence of the five senses.'

Naturally I allowed no hint of these reflections to appear to the two plain-clothes policemen. As for the rest of the setting, it certainly had its surprising elements; the idea struck me that I might have intruded on some ceremony in the midst of its meticulous course.

People talk about once-in-a-lifetime experiences as if every zeptosecond of your life wasn't a once-in-a-lifetime experience. You won't want to miss this – it's a once-in-a-lifetime experience! By going out to commune on a hill with some rare supermoon eclipse you're missing thousands of other once-in-a-lifetime experiences. Which is perfectly fine as long as you understand the choices you're making. And in so doing realise that no single experience is qualitatively better or worse than any other. One experience can only be different from another, and within *different* reside a million grades of difference.

I opened the folder lying on top of the stack of folders. I leafed through the various printouts, notebook pages covered in an untidy scrawl, pages ripped out of different books, receipts, shopping lists. I stopped short when I got to a red spiral-bound notebook, a little bigger than the size of an index card, which when I opened it contained not my lazy, curlicued handwriting but row after row of black ink scribbles made by the disorderly hand of the late Thomas Early.

40

V having trouble sleeping. We're both trying meditation. She's better at it than I am esp. the visualization part. I close my eyes and see darkness. She sees herself as Anubis. Who can compete w/ that? Nobodaddy.

Cemetery mailbox. Postal ghosts. Riven. Rubber shells of truckers' tires stranded by the side of road.

Horses grazing in flat fields of matted straw. Denuded sycamores barkless and leaf-stripped.

Spitting image. Spit and image. Essence and appearance.

What Happens Next Will Destroy You

If I took off your head, what would I find? Dangling ganglia, and all that implies. The stem of a stem. Ephemeral viscera, the glug of a stupid pump stupidly pumping, organs of sense that no longer make sense. Please press the pound sign to continue.

I have, unfortunate soul that I am, a poetical bent. The hew of a poet. The clean-and-jerk of a metaphor-making machine. You'll not find me in any of your constabularies, Mr. Smith. Triter as you mitre.

His voice unmatched at rating. Snaky throngs of the whips. Spatterdashed to the knee in mud. Larking over the newest gates in the country.

Cenotaph: a tomb-like monument to someone buried elsewhere, especially one commemorating people who died in a war.

No rule and ferule maintained his discipline.

You have to earn your grave. Working in an office is nothing more than a running start toward suicide. Leaving aside the inane repetition of pointless daily tasks, there's, God, there's the people. You have to talk to them. It's no use trying to avoid them, because the more you avoid them the more persistent they will become in their attempt to win you over or get you to open up.

The fourfold root of the principle of sufficient reason my ass.

Aldebaran (blue/red star in constellation of Taurus [Pleiades], c.f. G. de Nerval's Sylvie)

Falls drop by drop onto the bounceless floor.

Preponderance of roadside graves. In rural Indiana and in rural France. Difference is in France they're usually attached to a village church.

The typo in one of Nabokov's books. It was in French. The typo I mean. What if it became an obsession for the main character and his friends. Who may or may not be real. I forget which novel. Either *The Gift* or *Real Life*? Check. I recall that it was in both paperback editions. The older McGraw Hill and the newer Vintage International.

The best American novel of the 20th century is *Miss Lonelyhearts* by Nathanael West. By a long shot. Nothing else comes close.

The ants around here are insane.

Lost for words. Lots for words.

The Wine Experience, sez the Bible

One is reminded of Dostoevski's observation: "A man who bows down to nothing can never bear the burden of himself."

Much of modern philosophy has been skeptical of the possibility of knowledge independent of the physical senses, and Immanuel Kant gave this point of view its canonical expression: that the noumenal world may exist, but it is unknowable to humans. In Kantian philosophy, the unknowable noumenon is often linked to the unknowable thing-in-itself ("Ding an sich," which could also be rendered as thing as such or thing per se), although how to characterize the nature of the relationship is a question yet open to some controversy.

Eggs
Butter
Flour

Good-bye
Goodbye
G'bye

41

I've never seen the point in keeping a diary, but Thomas was a novelist, and apparently novelists like to record things that happen to them or thoughts that occur to them so as to consult said record during fallow periods, or sporadically to review the Amtrak of one's *pensées* as it ambles from station to station through the heartland of one's life, breaking down intermittently, running over milch kine and/or fair maidens strapped to the wobbly tracks. It's always been a mystery to me why America hasn't managed to develop a long-distance rail system unriddled with derangements. One of life's great pleasures is taking a night train across one or several borders.

There were pages and pages in his notebook, which I would enjoy reading instead of 'working' on my 'translation' — accompanied by a stab of melancholy, not least because he left signs of what he might have written next, and I would have liked to read what he might have written next. His solicitude about my insomnia notwithstanding, Thomas was not in the habit of talking about himself or asking about me. I think he assumed, as I did, that if something was bothering me I'd tell him. He knew about my insomnia, and apparently worried about it, or kept a record of it, because I complained about it. Meditation didn't help with that; medication did.

Of course I was better at meditation than he was, having had more practice, but I'm not sure I told him how much more practice I had. I can be a closed book when it comes to certain things. If I went off for a few weeks or a month to the Dhagpo Kundreul Ling temple, I wouldn't necessarily tell him where I was going/had been and didn't expect him to ask. And he didn't. That's how I roll, and to be fair, were Thomas to disappear for a few weeks or a month without telling me where or why, I wouldn't have asked about it either. But he never did, until he did for good.

The entries were undated, so I couldn't be sure when Thomas wrote them, though because he slipped the notebook in among my papers, which were probably sitting in a pile on top of my seldom-used printer, I could infer that either the entries were recent or that he'd recently wanted me to see the notebook.

And do what? That's what puzzled me. The last words of this particular entry (goodbye in three variations) shouldn't be taken as a me-directed parting note. This entry was from early on in the notebook, and so cannot have been or probably wasn't written in proximity to Thomas's leap of whatever. I was tempted to flip to the end and see if he'd left me any personal messages, but that would be cheating, and although I have done and been many things in my brief life, I do not cheat. I don't mean not ever, but in the vast preponderance of cases you can expect me to do you fair.

A contingency might arise in which I would be required to do you unfair, and in that instance I would also not let you know that I had done you unfair. So you may have been done unfair, and not know it, and maybe never know it, and for that I am truly not sorry. Were you to discover at some point that I had done you unfair, and you had pointed that out to me, I would be sorry, but I would be sorry that I got caught, not that I had done you unfair. I repeat that it is not my intention to do you unfair, and would in addition like to add that I am enjoying saying do you unfair repeatedly for reasons I am not at present able to articulate, but a contingency might arise in which, et cetera.

We used to spend hours playing each other records. I would play *Saxophone Colossus* and try to explain to the best of my understanding what was happening musically and why Thomas should savour Sonny Rollins's saxophone-playing as much as I did, and he would play me *Hex Enduction Hour* and try to explain to the best of his understanding what was happening musically and why I should savour Craig Scanlon's guitar-playing as much as he did. I don't remember now whether Thomas liked to characterise the Fall as punk or post-punk or its own *sui generis* thing. I get that categorisation is sometimes necessary, because it can provide a frame of reference, but my approach when dealing with an unfamiliar artist is first to listen, and listen again, and if possible listen again but in a different way (say, a live performance), and only then apply my critical apparatus. This sounds like aesthetic moralising, because that's exactly what it is. I am truly insufferable. No wonder Thomas killed himself.

As a result, I can no longer ask Thomas to explain his categories and subcategories to me. He was never cuter than when condescending to me. It was especially fun when I knew he was wrong, and he knew I knew he was wrong, and he kept going. Must be something blokes get from birth, this need to explain things they don't themselves fathom. To pretend to comprehend. To believe that someone else wants to learn what you don't know, and that that person wants you, and only you, to explain it to her. Not wanting to kill the inept exegete: that must be something like love.

42

I can't help you. I can't. It's all I can do not to actively hurt you. You'd think that would be easy, seeing that I don't know you or where you are or who you are, but you're wrong. Or I'm wrong in thinking that you'd think that. One of us is wrong. I will cause you pain. I already have, but you don't know it yet. You know about the pain, but you don't know who caused it. Or you think you know, but once again: wrong. I'm the source of the totality of emotional misery. Every little twinge of regret or remorse or bittersweet heartache you've felt is because of me. I did that. I've always done that. And I will continue to do that until time stops being a thing. Sorry.

When you examine the typologies of most creation myths, you find similarities. Some incidental, some coincidental, and some consistently the same in both form and content down to certain specific details (for example, the universality of flood-destruction narratives). Scholars have and will continue to argue the whys and wherefores of these contiguous threads (prevalence of regional floods? One catastrophic flood that remained in the collective memory? Symbolic of something else, like the submarine nature of nature post-fall, or at least post-Mark E. Smith?) but the threads don't care, the threads just *are*. It's foolish to conclude from these similarities that each of the creation myths springs from one ur-myth, but it's as foolish to dismiss as mere coincidence these contiguous threads. Things don't always happen for a reason. But sometimes they do.

If the whole body were an eye, where were the hearing? Today I felt like my whole body were an eye. I was suffering from what Thomas Early would call viniferous overconsumption aftermath syndrome. When things get weird, I often turn to alcohol. It's not an ideal solution, but when weird happens, the weird part of me happens. That's the part I fight like hell to keep anyone from seeing. That's the part that gets people killed.

I do not see why, but I continued my account without demanding an explanation. The girl, Temple, walked along the immense deserted beach, lost, hewing closely to the advancing scallops of wavelets, which wet periodically her bare feet.

An astonishing other thing: the more I read Thomas's journal entries, the less sense they make, or make to me, given what I know or thought I knew about him. In the pages I've been reading this morning, he cites *Luftkrieg und Literatur* in German ten times. Ten times in four pages. Now, it's not unordinary that he should quote Sebald, given that Max's effect on American intellectuals was even then at epidemic proportions, but I was under the impression he didn't know more than three words of German.

43

H2 had arrived back at Cap Ferret, but he'd left me alone. His spies must have reported that I'd been working, though I hadn't been. One of the perks about being a translator – I suppose this is true of any writer – is that no one can tell if you're working or not. As long as you're reading or writing something, it looks like you're working. I like reading and writing things, so it's easy to fake it.

En revanche, his lurking in the vicinage made it harder both to fake-work and real-work. I was, in a word, *distrait*, and spent not insignificant portions of my next few days sitting on my bed meditating – making japam, as Christopher Isherwood calls it in his enchanting sixties-era journal; the term is more properly spelled japa and refers to the recitation of a Sanskrit mantra, either spoken softly or within the reciter's mind, often accessorised with prayer beads.

A common mantra is the famous *aum mani padme hum*, the meaning of which is ambiguous but has something to do with the jewel in the lotus, a central feature of Tibetan Buddhism in particular. Typically you repeat this mantra one hundred and eight times, once each for the number of beads in the *japa mala*, or prayer beads. I never used prayer beads, and I never recited out loud. I almost never do anything the way you're supposed to. Sometimes I used a derivative variation of the mantra, and often I used no mantra and instead relied on a visualisation: of a lotus flower; of a mandala; of some recondite Tibetan deity.

On the fifth day of my sit-in, the hotel staff slipped a note on hyacinth-coloured paper under my door from H2 requesting my presence at dinner that evening. I thought I might plead the curse or calenture or just not fucking go, but on reflection I knew this would but delay the inevitable. H2 was not interested in my grims and megrims, he wanted value for money, and though I had delayed as long as possible the inevitable confession of my failure, the time had clearly come to own up. Plus, I figured my figure should make an appearance to appease his concupiscent cravings, if not his curiosity.

When I put in the effort I can make myself a presentable dinner guest. I slipped into apricot underwear, a thin dress of bronze-coloured silk, and thigh-high white boots. I pinked my fingernails. I did not take a shower, but I did run a brush through my blowsy hair. Though I was planning to let him down, there was, I thought, no reason I couldn't soften the blow by a strategic application of my glowing beauty.

What if antimatter or dark energy or whatever fabric the bulk of the universe is constructed from is a rubber-band ball of our unmade choices? What if that's why we can't see it, because there's an effectively infinite number of choices we could have made, but didn't, and the radiating subsets of each unmade choice spin complex gossamer strands of nothing, endlessly: repeating, dividing, lattice upon lattice, interstices within interstices, mesh over mesh; and that's what surrounds us in ring-straked circles from here to eternity?

I mean, if all else failed, we could always talk about *that* over dinner.

44

I canted sylphly into my seat in H2's dining room at the requested hour. We were being served by Morgan and his staff. The food – I don't remember the food. I'm sure it was amazing. The wine – ditto. I drank greedily, grasping the knop of my ornate crystal wine glass as if by some process of diffusion I might myself turn translucent. But I was too distracted by what H2 had to tell me, or rather to ask me, to take in much more than that. I didn't even get to broach the subject of my failed translation. Instead, he wanted me to see if my bitch twin sister would go to some fancy dress party in Paris with him.

You want to go on a date with my sister?

Not a date. I merely want to get to know her a little better. You and I will be working together for a long time, we will come to know each other's peccadillos, peeves, phobias, et cetera. Your sister on the other hand is a stranger to me.

And to me. I'd like to keep it that way, I said.

I have no experience of brothers or sisters. I've heard of sibling rivalry.

This has nothing to do with sibling rivalry. This is sibling identity theft. She stole my life. The life she's living – not that I envy her, I'm sure she's miserable, she was never any good at enjoying herself – was meant to be my life. I was the predestined celeb. She was the scholar.

A thing can be true and false at the same time, he said. Perhaps you wanted the life you have, he said. Perhaps you don't want the one she has. Or perhaps it's as you say. What's the difference?

Your lack of empathy is your emblematic character trait. Don't thank me.

Thank you, he said.

Surpassed, perhaps, by your inability to comprehend the words coming out of my mouth.

What words do you mean?

Was H2 fucking with me? I'm susceptible to being fucked with because I have a superior attitude towards everyone and everything. When you suspect everyone of stupidity, you can be made to look a fool by someone who's not as foolish as you think.

I wasn't going to call A to ask her to go to some costume ball with H2. In the first place: I never called A. She never called me. We didn't call each other. We didn't text. We communicated indirectly, through our parents, and once in a while (birthday, Christmas) via emotion-free email.

In the second place: I was beginning to suspect that H2 had no real interest in my (admittedly impossible) translation, and that he had lured me to his rickety sea prison to isolate me so that, whatever his designs, I would not be able to alert anyone. Except people who wouldn't care, like my parents. Did he know this about my parents? Was he that smart?

When he gave me the new phone I wasn't upset; I was relieved, because a ringing phone scares the hell out of me. No one who would call me could call me, which initially I thought was great. Great! Hardly anyone calls me, anyway, but now *no one* calls me. Still: OK. But I don't care in what hermetic solitude you reckon you live, it's not about people calling you, it's about you calling them. And you can't do that if you don't have your phone: not because you've got some easily hacked parental control on outgoing calls on your temporary phone, but because you don't have the contacts stored on your real phone. We have lost the ability to remember phone numbers. Like any data storage device, the brain deletes unused files in order to make room for more useful information. We don't need to remember phone numbers anymore. We scroll through a list of names and press call or some variation of call. Or we press text, or write a text, or tell our phone to write a text, or send a flurry of emoticons to express something like a sentiment without teeth, without eyes, without taste, without everything.

Quoi qu'il en soit, I was in the middle stages of a world-at-large connectivity withdrawal that had gradually grown more onerous. It's not that I wanted to call or text or write to anyone. It's that I was too markedly aware that I could not do so. I felt an uncanny narrowness, shut in a room or series of rooms without contact or the possibility of contact.

I want my phone back, I told H2.

That will be difficult, he replied.

I don't care. I want it back. By tomorrow at the latest. Or I will not continue to work on the translation you have not asked about. And I will certainly not ask my bitch twin sister anything on your behalf.

He sighed, though it sounded more like air escaping from a sealed tomb.

I will see what I can do, he said.

A bright point of pain pierced me in the upper right arm. I turned my head and saw Morgan extracting a syringe. The sound of H2's voice turned from a hiss to an underwater gurgle. Objects began to liquefy in front of me. I had the feeling of slipping under a warm wave of the collected tears of all women throughout history, and soon lost the ability to control my limbs.

Don't fight it, said H2 from the watery depths. Relax.

45

The original word for *sell* used to mean *give*, in what linguists are pleased to call prehistoric English. You can see how that could happen. You can see how anything could happen, if you don't pay attention. Most people, including me, do not pay attention. It is our chronic lack of attention that allows us to be surprised when predictable things happen.

I didn't get my phone back. I didn't get anything back. I got drugged and tied up, which in retrospect I should have seen coming. I was a victim of my chronic lack of attention. Actually, I was a victim of H2, the swine, but I was irked at myself for relaxing my habitual prudence in his presence.

I revived in a wine cellar, which I guessed to be H2's wine cellar, though because I had never been to his wine cellar and had no idea how long I'd been unconscious, I had to acknowledge was possibly a wine cellar in some other part of the country, or some other country. But my money, which I did not at that moment have access to, was on this being H2's wine cellar.

I had been administered some kind of paralysing agent, and could neither move nor feel my limbs. It was all I could do to lift my head slightly and peer down the length of me. I was strapped to a table, my arms stretched to the sides and restrained in leather bracelets attached to short metal chains. My legs were splayed in a similar fashion as far as the table would allow. I was naked except for my apricot silk panties, which would not have been my first choice had I known abduction and/or rape were in the offing when I dressed. Three bright lights of the type used in film production were focused on me so that I could not see beyond their penumbra. The heat from the lights was perfervid. I was sweating, despite the cellar itself being otherwise cold.

I don't have a problem being naked, or mostly naked, in front of strangers. The male gaze holds no terrors for me. But consent, implicit or explicit, is the first requirement in any scenario that entails getting my kit off. Whether I do it myself or it involves an elaborate art installation where I'm the bride stripped bare by her bachelors (random example that came to mind for no reason whatsoever), I have to say *yes*. It's a simple, hard-to-misinterpret word. Shades of doubt occur in OK, which is why OK is not enough. OK is what I say to my parents when they ask how I'm doing. OK is what I told Thomas Early when he asked if I'd go with him to see some noisome band at a place called the Cake Shop (which, confusingly, also sold cakes). OK is what I tell a crazy person, following a demand for my assessment of the crazy person's sanity phrased as *Tell me I'm not crazy!*

Not OK is what I would have said had I been able to say anything in my present situation. But the paralysis extended to my vocal cords, and I was currently unable to utter anything beyond a glurk of protest.

When you said the twin Vanessa eats the firebird, what did you mean?

It didn't sound like H2. It sounded more like Morgan, H2's private chef, which made sense considering his was the last face I had seen, and that he must be operating alongside or under the orders of H2.

The question was repeated with an undertone of menace. I did my best to respond.

Morgan? I asked. My voice sounded faraway and like a suffocating frog, but I managed to speak intelligibly.

Dr Morgan will ask the questions. You would do well to answer him. This was clearly H2's voice, though it seemed to come over an intercom or loudspeaker.

It's probably a sexual metaphor, I said, without knowing what I was saying.

Are you tired?

Yes.

Why did you never mention the apple the girl was eating?

What girl?

The young one. Temple. In French he said *la jeune Temple* but I think this is what he meant.

Yes, that's true, there was an apple, I said, thinking back.

I saw rubber-gloved hands holding a lancet advance towards my left hip and slice through the narrow band of fabric there. The panties fell slack, but pinioned as I was there hadn't been much left uncovered in the first place. I squinted sedulously into the lights to try to see a face. I was certain that if I could make eye contact with H2 (I felt sure it was him behind the gloves and the lancet) I could use the power of my crystalline gaze to get him to stop. In fact I'd never been more certain of anything. I would stop whatever was happening from happening. I would project my personality through the twin suns of my eyes and glut the room with a brighter light than the stage rig ringing the table. The gloved hand reached towards the sliced fabric and pulled it away towards my right hip, revealing my pubic fleece – at which point it stopped and dropped the corner of my undergarment, withdrawing into the lights. I knew what had happened. My power was growing stronger. I was able to see through the klieg lights, which were not klieg lights but twenty-watt bulbs compared to my own luminescence. The sunly emanant glow was now sourced not just from the orbs in my head but the origin of the world, *L'Origine du monde*, to make a painterly reference, my blinding cunt, which was both drawing from and reflecting the energy of the lights in the room, and in every other room; the energy of every star in the universe; an unbounded, perpetual, expanding energy that consumed me as it radiated, uncontrollably. I was no longer paralysed. I slipped my girly bonds. I rose up off the table and progressed towards the retreating figures at the back, who I could now see too clearly, meaning that I could see through them, through their bones, but as a result could not identify them. Which didn't matter anymore. I was calm. I was serenity itself. The lights in the room imploded resoundingly as I stepped forward. Pop. Pop. Pop. Someone spoke. It may have been me. *Fiat lux*, said the voice. And there was – no light. Everything went dark, and I was back on the table, alone, cold and exhausted from the effort of generating the light of a million suns. I struggled to stay conscious, but I wasn't afraid, not anymore. Curious, sure, but not afraid. So I passed right back out.

46

I woke in my bed, in my apartment in New York. It was dark. I reached to the bedside table, where I always kept my phone. My phone was there. The screen read 02.42. The date was the second of December, but . . . How was I home?

Something had awakened me. A sound, like a thunder-clap to my sleeping ears, but likely no more than a muffled thump in waking life. I got up to investigate. I noticed that my apricot panties had been crudely stapled together at the left hip. I threw on the silk robe lying at the foot of my bed and padded round the loft space barefoot, using my phone as a flashlight. Nothing was out of place. That in itself was unsettling. Something is always out of place at my place. I leave books and papers piled everywhere, empty coffee cups, glasses of water, bottles of Singani. I never sweep or vacuum. Someone does that for me, but they don't come when I'm out of town; I was sure I had texted them to say don't come, but *someone* had come, *someone* had straightened up. I looked for my laptop, which was on my desk as usual, sleeping, the soft white logo on its back glowing and dimming, glowing and dimming, like a thing with breath (but no feathers; no need).

I sat down in my desk chair and opened the laptop. The last entry was Chapter 45, and ended with the words *So*

I passed right back out. Which is odd because you don't remember passing out, do you? You wake up whenever later, knowing that at some point you passed out, but you don't, except in certain cases, like panic attacks or heatstroke, think to yourself *I'm passing out.* You pass out. The definition of losing consciousness is that you are not conscious. You cannot be conscious of the fact of your unconsciousness. Unless subconsciously – but you wouldn't say something like *I subconsciously remember passing out,* or *my subconscious remembers passing out, but I don't,* because that's, well, that's just stupid.

If I didn't type those words, who did? And more to the point, when? Because although I remember every detail of Chapter 45 with painful clarity, I have no memory of writing Chapter 45. I don't believe H2 or Dr Morgan had the talent to mimic my voice so expertly, nor could they have known or described what I was feeling with such accuracy.

I shut the lid of the laptop and headed back to bed. At some point – but at what point exactly? – you're going to realise that either I did not shut the lid of the laptop and head back to bed, or that I wrote about shutting the lid of the laptop and heading back to bed sometime after the event, or that I wrote about it *avant la lettre* and shut the lid and went to bed. It stands to reason that I could as easily have written Chapter 45 sitting at my desk wearing nothing but my stapled-together underwear, and you would have no way of knowing whether or not I was telling the truth. I think I've mentioned before, but am at present too knackered to check, that I always tell the truth.

Which is how you know I'm telling you the truth.

47

The next morning, or later that same morning, I got up, showered (!), changed into my usual T-shirt/jeans combination, made a double espresso, and sat down at my desk to more scrupulously probe the mystery of my reappearance. Or the reappearance of the world. Because I hadn't disappeared, I'd known where I was the whole time, or thought I did.

Next to my laptop was the folder of material I'd had with me in Cap Ferret, including Thomas Early's notebook. Next to the folder was my heavily mutilated copy of *Souvenirs du triangle d'or*. Next to the Robbe-Grillet book was its most recent translation, by Breunn. Behind that was a pile of random Not Michel Houellebecq novels in both French and English.

The phone rang. It was Not Michel Houellebecq's American editor.

Where have you been? I've been trying to reach you for days! She sounded frantic, like she hadn't slept, like maybe she'd been held captive and nearly ravined by her insane author.

I've been with your insane author, I replied. Who took away my phone. And my internet.

Oh thank God. I've been fielding calls from everyone. His French publisher, his French agent, the president of France. Does France have a president or a prime minister? Anyway. Everyone.

Deal's off, by the way, I said. No amount of money is worth what I've been through.

Oh, come now, Vanessa. She drawled the third syllable of my name as if exhaling a plume of smoke.

He's a pain in the rear, she said, no one's gonna argue that, but we all have our eccentricities. And we both know it's not about the money. I don't suppose he's there with you now?

I realised: she had no idea where he was. She wasn't worried about me, or whether I quit or did not quit translating his unwritten new novel. She was worried about him. About H2. That loathsome, spineless, question mark of a man. More precisely, she was worried that she'd get in trouble for losing him. And would consequently be fired, lose her house, end up on the street begging for quarters by the subway entrance. It was as plain as the words written on her face, which though I couldn't see them I knew were: *lacrimae rerum.*

No. Try Cap Ferret. That's where we were last.

Cap Ferrat? Why on earth would he be in Cap Ferrat? He hardly ever leaves Paris, and when he does it wouldn't be for some Côte d'Azur playground.

Not Cap Ferrat. Cap Ferret. Near Bordeaux. His summer house.

Wedding bells of laughter on the other end of the line. I held the phone away from my ear for a beat, annoyed.

I'm sure if H had a summer house in Cap *Ferret* (her pronunciation was roughly five thousand nautical miles west of the mark) I would know about it.

I'm on to the whole game, I said. I know everything. I know that H is not-H. I know he pays a guy to do his public appearances. And the real guy, let me tell you, H2? He's a monster. He drugged me and tied me up, you know.

The line went dead. I looked at the phone's screen: call failed.

You can say that again, I told it.

When the phone rang again I almost didn't answer.

48

S'il vous plait, ne raccrochez pas, je vous expliquerai tout, said a querulous and familiar voice on the other end of the line.

H1? I asked, tentatively. C'est vous?

Je ne connais pas cet H1. Je suis H. Le vrai H. Le seul H. Peut-être pas le seul. Mais je suis Ne Pas Michel Houellebecq, écrivain. Je le jure.

Mais je vous ai vu—

J'étais drogué! he interrupted. Cet — espèce de crétin qui me remplaçait m'a drogué et — et — je ne sais pas ce qui s'est passé après avec vous, mais moi, je me suis reveillé dans un entrepôt vide et évidemment abandonné. Ce qui paraît être une usine en bordure de mer — j'ai entendu les mouettes, j'ai senti l'eau salée — comme en témoignent les treuils, câbles, chaînes, et poulies de toutes tailles que l'on distingue vers le haut du cadre. C'était peut-être une conserverie de poisson.

Peut-être. Continuez.

J'étais enchaîné à un truc, très lourd, comme un radiateur mais plus grand. Je ne pouvais pas bouger. Il n'y avait pas de fenêtre sauf au plafond, très, très haut, qui ne laisse passer qu'un rayon de soleil de temps en temps, très rarement. Tout était gris, tout était sombre. Je souffrais dans l'obscurité je ne sais pas combien de temps. Je m'endors, je me reveille; et puis comme par magie il y avait une *soupe dégueulasse devant moi. Je ne vois personne, mais voilà. La nourriture.*

I had let him babble, unable to decide whether this was another con, another trick, or whether H1 was telling the truth. It made more sense than anything else I'd heard so far today, but that wasn't saying much.

Dites-moi, I said. *Vous n'êtes jamais allé à Cap Ferret? Près de Bordeaux?*

Oui, c'est possible. Pourquoi?

Peu importe. Pourquoi vous m'appelez, M. H?

Parce que je me méfie de tout le monde sauf vous en ce moment. Je viens d'échapper à un enfer, un véritable enfer. Et — et — j'ai besoin de votre aide.

Uh-huh. En fait je suis très occupée, aujourd'hui en particulier.

Please, he said. H1 didn't switch to English, but I'm tired of trifling with you, the non-Francophone reader.

If you're anxious to know what you missed in the above exchange, I'll summarise: *Help, I'm the real H, that other guy drugged me and I woke up in an abandoned warehouse or possibly an old fish canning factory (which he likened to hell, though I don't think he was being literal) judging from the equipment and the smell and the seagulls. I've just now escaped. You're the only one I trust, you have to help me.*

All of which you'd expect anyone impersonating H to say. But I wasn't going to write the guy off. I don't write guys like that off like that. Or, I do, but not this time, because though I affected not to buy his bluster, and told him I was too busy to concern myself with fairy tales, I was never not going to see him. I was too spooked by recent experience, which slotted closely (drugging, kidnapping) with his story, and too curious to sit this one out. I gave him my address and ended the call.

I was reminded of a quote from Renan: *complication is anterior to simplicity*. I walked over to the Hilma af Klimt painting I'd acquired long before her ascent to Art Heaven, one of her *Paintings for the Temple*, the Swan series, No. 11. It's one of the most ravishing paintings I've seen in my life, but there's something forlorn about its composition that I have never been able to place.

This should be good, I said out loud to the ghost of Thomas Early, sitting in his usual chair. He nodded and smiled, as he did when listening or pretending to listen to me.

You're right, it's not there anymore. Good job noticing things, Ms Temple! I sold it back to the dealer. You know how your favourite band is partly your favourite band because no one else knows about it – like that's an actual key component of your enjoyment, the idea that the band is your secret, and that you can share that secret or not with people of your choosing, but that otherwise the wider world is ignorant of its existence? That's kind of how I feel about everything. I'm either ahead of the curve or the curve doesn't exist, is the way I like to look at life. On those increasingly rare occasions when I look at life.

49

H1 arrived about twenty minutes later. I first saw him at the corner of my street, crossing against the light, and soon thereafter heard the gentle jingle of my intercom. I buzzed him in and he appeared, attoseconds later, in the vestibule, as dishevelled and out of sorts as you'd expect, as he was when I last saw him. Before he passed out in his tomato soup.

Do you have anything to drink? he said, by way of intro-duction or reintroduction.

I motioned for him to follow me to the kitchen, where I mixed up a pitcher of Singani Bloody Marys:

2 OZ SINGANI 63
2 OZ FRESH TOMATO JUICE
.25 OZ FRESH LEMON JUICE
4 DASHES TABASCO SAUCE
1 DASH WORCESTERSHIRE SAUCE
1 BAR SPOON HORSERADISH
3 PINCHES PEPPER
1 PINCH SALT

BLOODY MARY

SPONSORED CONTENT

STIR INGREDIENTS. POUR INTO A
HIGHBALL GLASS WITH ICE. GARNISH WITH
VEGETABLES YOU'RE IN LOVE WITH.

Multiply that by eighteen, because I made a lot. I pulled some mouldy Cantal wrapped in paper (not wasting the good stuff on an impostor, or imposture, or this guy) from the fridge and laid it on a plate with an open box of stale water crackers and a few slices of prosciutto. H1 ate automatically, as if he didn't even taste his food (a hanging offence in France, but we weren't in France, so I let him slide), and drank his Bloody Mary quickly, as if trying to steady his nerves, or as if trying to convince me he was trying to steady his nerves. I watched him carefully while simulating not watching him carefully. He noticed, as I'd hoped he would.

This other man, this—

I call him H2, I said. He claims to be you. He says you're an actor he's hired as front man for his literary output.

But this is preposterous!

Improbable. But not impossible.

I am, I have . . . how does one prove that one is oneself?

Why did you want to hire me to translate your new book?

I told you, I read your translation of . . . of . . . He dropped his head, defeated.

My editor said you were good, he said. *Too good for you* was how she put it. I cannot judge the quality of anything translated into or from French. I'm a writer. I only need to know one language.

Did you expect me to translate a book you haven't yet written? I asked him.

What? Of course not. The new novel is finished. It's about—

I don't care what it's about, I interrupted.

To translate a book that hasn't been written, he mused. That would be impossible.

Turns out. Listen, why not call her, then? Your editor. She rang here not long ago, looking for you.

I don't trust her. She's probably in on it. I don't trust anyone. Not yet.

You never answered my question. Why did you pick me to translate your new book?

It's difficult to explain. Something about you—

I'm not a fan, I said. Of your writing, I mean. Your editor should have told you that.

She did. Naturally this made me more determined to hire you. Also she said that you were very . . . alluring.

You thought maybe I'd fuck you to get the job?

I thought maybe this was possible.

Have you looked in the mirror recently?

My appearance has in the past not proved a barrier when it comes to attracting amatory partners.

I think you're full of shit, I said. I think you only called me because you still think you have a shot.

No, I swear—

You gave me a plot description of *Souvenirs du triangle d'or* when I asked what your new book was about. Back when I was at all interested.

I have no memory of doing that. I have never read this book. Robbe-Grillet, correct?

Correct.

He was an old pervert. He only wrote to get off.

Says the old pervert.

Yes, but I write for other reasons too.

So did Robbe-Grillet.

I like some of his earlier books. Before he got into sadomasochism.

What else can you tell me about H2?

Who is H2?

The other you. The guy you claim drugged you and took your place. You must have done some digging.

I've been free for maybe three hours. No digging.

He was holding something back. It didn't matter just then, but I could tell he knew more about H2 than he was saying. Even if, as he claimed, and as I could well believe (having watched him pitch forward into his tomato soup), he hadn't managed to see the man who replaced him, he had ideas. Which for now he was unwilling to share.

He finished off his Bloody Mary with impressive speed. I'd only drunk a major third of mine.

Let's refill your drink, shall we? I said. I got up and fetched the pitcher off the kitchen counter.

He sniffled: copiously; waterishly. Tears of gratitude, I suppose. Or maybe he was a junkie going through the early phases of withdrawal. Either way, I had to cut it short.

No crying in my house. That's my cardinal rule.

He wiped his face on the edge of his frayed olive-green herringbone blazer.

I'm sorry.

Don't apologise. Just don't cry.

OK.

I'm not going to sleep with you, either.

OK.

Stop saying 'OK'. It's getting on my nerves.

But you do it all the time, he whined.

OK.

Did I tell you I'm wearing sixty-dollar boxer shorts?

50

When A and I were very young, maybe five or six years old, we were inseparable. What I remember best about her, despite the years of betrayal and ingratitude, despite the different directions our careers and lives and hair colour took, is that closeness. It's what blooms involuntarily whenever her name – her real name, not the absurd stage name she took to obscure her origins – comes to mind, whether because someone has spoken it or because I've seen it written somewhere, in an email from my parents.

The things you do, the person you are at five or six years old, in some ways these things and that person define you for the rest of your life. You may not remember what you had for dinner last night, but you will always remember the first time your grandfather rubbed a buttercup on your chin or your nose (though you may not remember why; sense memories often do not require context to recall, which is what makes them stronger). You remember the sky was fair and the sun was strong, though it was morning, and the crab apple tree in the back garden was not yet in flower or leaf. You remember the ugly pink dress with white stockings and clunky shoes your sister wore as she tried to hide behind you and away from Grand-père and his aggressive buttercupping, because you were dressed identically, and felt as uncomfortable as she did in what I suppose was our Sunday best. Angelica was more farouche when she was younger, more awkward and untamed and, well, like me, before the changes rung by adolescence drew us down separate paths. You remember these things. Even at the time you somehow know you're going to remember these things. But that may just be me imposing my will on the palimpsest of the past.

These would have been my maternal grandparents, because they lived in Neuilly just north of the Bois de Boulogne and were easier to visit than my father's parents, who were somewhere in the Auvergne, which is like living in Kansas to a French person. Except a Kansas that's three or four hours away by car or train from Paris, as opposed to, say, twenty-one hours by car or a three-hour flight from New York City. Scale means naught to a five- or six-year-old girl, though. Any distance that required the use of a car or train or plane was identical, and intolerable, except on special occasions. So we did not often visit my paternal grandparents, except at Christmas, which made those occasions the more special, because where my father's parents lived in the Auvergne was at an elevation that got a lot of snow round Christmas. Although my grandfather was Jewish, we celebrated Christmas with him, partly out of some assimilationist impulse, mostly because my father did not hold tightly to his religious or ethnic identities, to my grandfather's muted disappointment (my grandmother wasn't Jewish, but was firmly secular in outlook, and took no position on the matter of holidays or holy days). Grand-père prized his lineage; his own grandparents were consanguineous in some degree to Alfred Dreyfus, and my grandfather as a boy, though born and raised in Paris, was both a Communist and a member of the French resistance in World War II, a lot of which was based in the Auvergne, close to the border with Vichy. After the war he met my grandmother, née Gauvin, and decided to stay, ignoring the often overtly anti-Semitic attitude of his rustic neighbours, who however could not too openly object to the presence of an actual hero of the Maquis; he bought a house and some land and raised cows and a few chickens on a scant farm which had in addition a paddock where a senescent mule wandered in its traces, and a walled orchard where apple and pear trees grew in untended abundance.

I couldn't bear to leave my fallen comrades, he used to say, explaining his decision not to return to Paris, and I have no reason to doubt his affection for his dead wartime friends. His tiny *hameau* (unmentioned on maps) was close to the Dhagpo Kundreul Ling temple, which is how I discovered it. He was in charge of a dinky museum of the resistance in a nearby village called Saint-Gervais-d'Auvergne, but its hours were irregular and the museum even when we were young was unfrequented. My father got the hell out as soon as he could, but in later years he sentimentalised his agrestic youth.

Christmas snow is magic at that age – especially at that age, before you get what snow is, or maybe when you get better than anyone else what snow is/is not. Snow is not crystallised water, or some other scientific nonsense. Snow is elemental; it cannot be reduced, only accumulated, played with and in and around. You make angels in snow. They're not real angels but they are real snow angels. You make snowmen from snow. They're not real men but they are real snowmen. You make snowballs and snowforts and snowbrows and snowsnot and snowfeet and snowhounds and snowsnows and snowsnowsnows and more snow. When it is snowing it has always been snowing and when the snow has stopped it has never been snowing. The snow is just there, on the ground, whorling and eddying round the woodpile and the gate and the plane trees and the firs and your sister. All sound is muffled in snowmute.

In the spring, in Paris, my father would sometimes take us to the Montparnasse cemetery to leave flowers on the grave of our ancestor Captain Dreyfus, though I spent more time lingering by the graves of Baudelaire, Serge Gainsbourg and Simone de Beauvoir (Sartre shares a headstone with her, but I had less interest in paying homage to him). My mother's mother was of Berber origin, from Oran in Algeria; she was a novelist, a contemporary and friend of Assia Djebar, with whom she shared a feminist outlook and an ambivalence about the French language and its colonial past in North Africa. She married a British civil servant, a minor aristocrat who ended up serving as ambassador to France in the sixties. My parents were both educated at the Normale sup' in Paris, which is where they met. The way these two people from very different social and ethnic backgrounds found in each other soulmates deserves a book of its own, but not everything that deserves a book of its own gets a book of its own, despite appearances.

Here is a picture of Christmas snow in the Auvergne:

51

In a far corner of my Auvergnat grandparents' garden stood an enormous fir tree, maybe fifty metres tall (in my imagination), with graceful, sweeping boughs that harboured in their piny depths barn owls and big, handsome European scrub jays. Pine cones the size of pineapples lay scattered in the snow under the tree. Next to the tree was the woodpile, gathered from the bosky environs, covered in a waterproof tarp, the logs split and ready for the fireplace, stacked on pallets to keep them dry. Except the pallets were always too low, and the snow always too high, and the logs got wet and had to dry next to the fire, and, when they were dry enough to go in, they hissed and crackled on the cinders like a pantomime witch.

We had snowshoes but I hated using them. I preferred to walk outside in my boots and try to build a path forward using my lower body, as the snow swallowed me up to my waist. A would follow closely, taking advantage of the path I pioneered (how I wish I had picked up on these early clues!) to reach the woodpile with far less effort. We helped load each other up with firewood and trudged back to the front door, banging on the glass of the door with our bobble-hatted heads until someone let us in. Someone always let us in, with undue fuss and admonitions about tramping snow on the carpet or the rugs or the hardwood floors, brushing the snow off our clothes and ridding us of any evidence that snow existed. I didn't mind. I was at an age where I found everyone both mildly annoying and mildly amusing at the same time.

Some things I liked better than others. *Pain perdu* in the morning. Hot chocolate at any hour. *The man who never alters his opinion is like standing water, and breeds reptiles of the mind.* Oh, and when the cheese truck came by, which it did no matter the weather every Friday evening, I was allowed to go with A and pick which cheese we wanted, after being instructed which cheese we wanted and given the necessary funds – back then it was francs but I cannot tell you how many francs because my brain long ago stopped converting prices from francs to euros, unlike my parents, who still do, and not-secretly long for and maybe expect the collapse of the European Union and the return of the franc in their lifetimes.

The bread truck I found less exciting. I don't know why. You need both to exist, patently, bread and cheese – and meat, too. My favourite meat was wild boar sausage, which could be found in abundance in the Auvergne (still can). My grandparents died, within a year of each other, when I was at *lycée*. I didn't go to their funeral, because it had been discovered two years earlier on the death of my mother's father that I cannot control my laughter at oppressively sombre events, and when I visit the area to go to the temple, I never stop by their old house. My memory cottage keeps my data disorderly and waterlogged, which is the way data should be kept. Revisiting the past in any other than a Proustian sense — that is to say, going back to places where one has, at great cost and over a long expanse of time, created and stored a memory — is worse than worthless, it is harmful, not just to one's sense of self but to the warp and woof of reality itself.

I write to kill the past, but it's a moving target, and I go too slow.

52

The problem with H1 was that he was exactly the way you would expect Not Michel Houellebecq to be, look, talk, act, drink, et cetera. Which is how Not Michel Houellebecq's hired double would be, right? I was left with choosing between two equally unlikely and bizarre possibilities. We were neck-deep into the third bottle of Singani when I decided to (for now) choose H1. Probably because choosing him would make the last several weeks of my life a little more explicable. I had been duped by a brilliant lunatic whose aims were unclear; I had not blindly followed a charlatan who drugged and abused me, and whose aims were all too clear.

I drug and abuse myself on the regular, let's not lose sight of this unsightly fact. But how I choose to destroy my body is my business. You don't get to superimpose on my own self-destructive tendencies your power trips or sad Sadean fantasies. Unless I give you explicit permission or, e.g., beg you to spank me senseless, you are not allowed to touch me. Or talk to me. Or look at me, for that matter. If I'm in a bad mood and you look at me the wrong way, I might kick in your teeth. It happens.

Other times, as when dealing with a serial harasser like H1, I'll let it pass for a while, because I'm mildly interested to see how long he can keep it up. If you see what I did there.

The state of the world will be precisely what it was before as to outward form. It is now allowable to enter intelligently into the mysteries of the faith.

In 1755 an earthquake destroyed Lisbon and forty thousand people died in the ensuing tidal wave, landslide, uncontrollable fire and General Panic. It took place on All Saints' Day and could be felt from Scotland to Asia Minor. Because of the religious significance of the day, and the fact that many people were in church when it happened, you can probably guess that the usual rebarbative opportunists promoted the usual apocalyptic scenarios.

But that was not the apocalypse. It wasn't even *an* apocalypse. It was a disaster. Surveying my own life and comparing it to the earthquake of 1755 always makes me feel better. My life is not a disaster. It's got its kinks, but I've killed far fewer than forty thousand people. To my knowledge, I've only killed one, and that one is more me plashing in a mire of guilt than an actual provable killing. Still. A kill's a kill. Any time I start to feel superior to someone like H1 slobbering over my Bloody Marys and my cheese and trying with his miniature claw-hands to straighten what remains of his steel-wool hair, I check myself. He's probably never killed anyone. He may have wanted to kill someone, he certainly has written about killing people. He's killed himself, in his own books, if it's him (here, in my apartment, I mean, not in his books, where when he appears as a character he's not himself but not *not* himself, either).

There's another possibility, H1 said, slurping from his twentyteenth Bloody Mary.

That neither I nor H2 are Not Michel Houellebecq, he said.

Sure, I said. Metatextual talk bores me, tbh.

Not Michel Houellebecq may not exist, he said.

I'm not that lucky, I said. Which was a lie, because I am that lucky. I don't like admitting it, especially in front of possibly non-existent cretins.

53

This talk of killing: stupid. I'm about peace and love, man. I look forward to the collapse of *rentier* capitalism as much as the next girl. I can do without any of the commodities I have. I'd be happy in a cabin in an isolated area. Maybe Newfoundland. I've always liked the sound of that place. When you come from a graveyard like Europe, the attraction of a relatively new culture cannot be overstated. In the room the women come and go, talking about death again. Jules Laforgue. *Graveyards*. 'Le cimitière marin'. 'Elegy Written in a Country Churchyard'. 'The Dead'. *Donner la mort*. Ask not for whom the bell tolls, ask who do you have to pay, and how much, not to have it rung.

Several drinks later, I watched H1 stumble out of my bathroom and slump onto my cream-coloured fainting couch. He looked like what death wanted people to think death looked like. He looked like life, or what life does to you if you're careless, or even if you're careful. Most of us are careful, to a point. *Clarity is overrated*, I once heard in an AA meeting I attended involuntarily. The remark was meant as a joke, the result of a misfired impulse towards irony. But I didn't take it as a joke. I took it seriously. I thought about it a lot.

Clarity. Do I enjoy clarity, or do I run screaming from any room where it's kept on display? Depends on the situation. On balance I prefer clarity, perhaps because *true* clarity is so difficult to achieve. Too often my brain is like a hemispheric bottle crammed with cotton balls, whether dead sober or cold drunk or grounded by chemicals.

I brought H1 another Bloody Mary, half-full, because though I didn't care about wine-dark stains on my sea-foam couch, I wanted him to think that I cared, so that he would either take care or deliberately spill his drink on my couch because that's what Not Michel Houellebecq might do if he was in a mood. Either way I would be interested in the result. In the event, he didn't notice my pretence of care, or if he noticed didn't himself care, as he drank the half-glass in one long draught and held out the glass for more, wiping his mouth with his sleeve.

I didn't refill his glass. I took it from him and set it on my coffee table. I sat down on the ottoman opposite him without a word. Just stared at him. I know not what I wanted to happen. Maybe I wanted him to do more to convince me that he was H, or maybe I wanted to catch him out and determine for sure that he was not H, or both, or neither. I filled my glass and sipped contemplatively, watching him watch me drink. The sole item on his mind's agenda was alcohol. Because I sometimes enjoy being cruel for no real reason, I decided to wait a while before giving him what he wanted.

My phone rang. I checked the screen. My parents. I don't ever want to speak to my parents. Not because I dislike them but because I have less-than-nil to say, and the resultant conversations are forced and weather-based; but I particularly did not want to speak to my parents now. I let the call go to voicemail. It rang again immediately. This was unusual. My parents are not persistent. They are perhaps the least persistent people I know.

You going to get that? slurred H1.

I stared at my screen, willing it to stop ringing. It did not. I walked over to the window, where I could delude myself that H1 wouldn't overhear me.

54

Vanessa? said my mother. Though she's fluent in both French and English, she was brought up speaking mostly English, and so we usually speak English. Her accent is irredeemably posh.

Maman? I said.

It's about your sister, said my mother.

What about her?

She's missing.

What does that mean, 'missing'? I said. She's never not missing. It's normal not to hear from her for months.

This is different. She sent a letter.

You mean an email?

No. A letter. It's her. It's her handwriting. No one has seen her since her film premiere last week. She says that she's run away with an Italian count, and that she doesn't want us to fret, but that she's finished with acting, through with the lot, and probably won't be in contact for a long time.

An Italian cunt?

Count.

I shrugged. If I was a smoker, but then again no.

Vanessa?

I'm here.

What should we do?

About what?

I watched H1 help himself to the bottle of Singani, pouring a sloshy glassful, neat, with unsteady hands. I wondered whether his hands were always unsteady. Usually with topers their hands get more steady when they're toping, but with H1 his hands never improve.

About your sister. You have to talk to her.

The noumenon is a posited object or event that is known (if at all) without the use of the physical senses. The term noumenon is generally used in contrast with, or in relation to, the term phenomenon, which refers to anything that can be apprehended by, or is an object of, the physical senses. In Platonic philosophy, the noumenal realm was equated with the world of ideas known to the philosophical mind, in contrast to the phenomenal realm, which was equated with the reality as perceived via the physical senses, as known to the uneducated mind.

Why do I have to talk to her?

Because you're the only person she'll listen to, my mother said.

Even if that were true, it doesn't answer my question.

She's lost her mind, Vanessa. Giving up her career? And for some dubious count who runs a chemical company?

My blood did not freeze, nor did my heart skip a beat, but there was a sensation in my stomach that could fairly be described as sinking.

What was that last part?

She mentioned that he was the CEO of a large chemical corporation based here in Paris, in addition to being an

Italian count, though we cannot find his name in the red book or anywhere else.

The red book?

The *Annuario della Nobiltà Italiana*. Or *Debrett's Peerage*, or any of the other directories.

That's because he's not a count. He's not at all what he claims. He's a fabulist.

You know him?

I've met him. Yes.

And you say he's a criminal? But Vanessa, you must do something!

I didn't say he was a criminal. Have you tried calling her yourself?

She changed her number. Temple can't find her. Or so she claims.

Temple—

Her assistant. And we tried Eva, same result.

Eva—

The actress. Her best friend, or supposedly. Also that one with the blue hair, what's her name, Léa?

Didn't we go to school with Léa?

Maybe the same school, but I think she's a few years younger.

Ouch. How am I supposed to get A's new number if you can't get it?

In her letter she specifies that you already have it, and that you alone have it. And further, that she'll only talk to you.

Interesting.

That's what she wrote.

Maman, please know, I'm not questioning what you've said. But Angelica and I haven't spoken in a long time.

I know, dear, but we're worried sick.

You're always worried sick.

With you two girls, it's no wonder!

The call was falling into maternal banality, which was a sign of how serious the problem was. My mother was rarely banal except when genuine emotion was called for, at which point she turned into a fount of truisms. It was one of the qualities I liked best about her.

I'll talk to her, I said. I'm sure it's a caprice. Or a joke.

I fail to see the humour.

I didn't say it was a good joke. I'll ring you as soon as we've spoken. In the meantime, try not to repine. How's Papa?

Oh. He's, well, you know, he's your father. Same as ever.

It was my turn to repine. How bad?

What do you mean?

How bad is he? Can he remember your name? Does he know his?

Whatever would give you the idea that—

Can I talk to him? Is he there?

He's sleeping, Vanessa. It's late.

All right. You get some sleep too. That's an order.

Oui, mon capitaine. Her tone brightened. I don't think she expected to talk me into calling A so easily. I was a little surprised, myself, at my willingness to do what I hadn't bothered to do for years. The events of the past few weeks had unmoored me.

I hung up and turned to H1.

The bastard's taken off with my sister, I said. He's posing as an Italian count.

Does he also own a chemical company? asked H1.

How do you know about the chemical company?
This is a dangerous man.
You do know him then.
I should think so. He's my brother.

55

Of course H2 was H1's brother. *Of course* he was. The only way that could not be true was if nothing was true. And some things are true. Aquinas proved that a few years back. That H2 was H1's brother made sense and helped restore balance to the universe. But doubts immediately crowded forward. First off, the two of them didn't look anything alike.

You don't look anything alike, I said.

Half-brother, said H1. We had the same father but different mothers. My father left my mother to be with his. Then he died. For a long time his mother did not tell him about my existence, but when I became famous, it was inevitable he would find out.

It's not your fault, I said, reflexively, without considering in any detail the matter of blame in H1's relations.

He's insane, H1 said. He pretends to be many different people. He runs a chemical company, he's a big Hollywood producer, he's an Italian count, he's the head of the largest French exporter of wine, he's an architect. You get the idea. But what makes this more than just silliness is that he believes himself to be these people, consecutively and sometimes simultaneously.

So he's not pretending.

No.

Because you said he pretends, I said.

I misspoke. Or maybe he is pretending. It's not possible to know for sure.

Your own brother drugged you and dragged you away. And then replaced you, claiming to be you.

So it would appear, he said.

That's messed-up.

Yes.

What do you intend to do about it?

Nothing.

You can't do nothing.

It's not possible to do something, he said. I have tried. He always has the advantage of me because he knows how life works and he's convincing. He's a salesman. That's his real talent. He sells people an idea of himself.

Is there money in that?

If people believe you are the head of a large chemical corporation in Paris, you can get away with a lot. It's curious, too.

What's curious? I asked.

He has a bizarre fascination with sadomasochism. The same as Robbe-Grillet, except he acts out his fantasies.

Yes, I was on the receiving end, no pun intended, or maybe pun intended, I'm not sure yet, of one of his fantasies.

I sighed. I knew that given what I'd learned and what I knew from my own experience, I would have to undertake the one action on earth I did not want to undertake. Besides drink California wine, I mean.

I was going to have to save my bitch twin sister from herself, and from H2, or both.

We have to do something, I said.

But I'm telling you it's not possible, he said. You cannot challenge him. By the time you find him he will have assumed a new identity and somehow you will end up paying his bills for him.

Because he outwitted you doesn't mean he can outwit me. I'm sure you'll agree, you're not good at . . . well, you know.

H1 nodded sadly. Yes. I know.

And because you're more familiar with the terrain, so to speak, much as I scout the idea, you'll have to come with me.

He was horrified.

I'd prefer not to.

I shrugged.

Fine by me, I said in English.

Va-t-en, I said in French.

You don't have to go home but you can't stay here, I said in cliché.

OK, he said. He looked sad, as anyone except Thomas Early would, at the prospect of leaving my comfortable apartment.

May I make a phone call before I go? he asked.

Sure, I said. I can be reasonable, I said.

56

He knocked on my bedroom door about five minutes later, as I was throwing some clothes into my rucksack. His face was whiter than usual.

No joy? I asked.

This time he has gone too far, he said.

His hands were shaking, despite or I guess because of the alcohol.

Meaning? I asked.

He has taken over my bank accounts and credit cards. I have to prove to the bank that I am who I am. In the meantime the bank will do nothing. And I can do nothing.

You have any cash on you?

He took my wallet when — he took my wallet. I don't have any cash, I don't have my ATM card, I don't have my credit cards. And even if I did he's locked me out of the accounts, cancelled the cards and had new ones issued.

Sounds like you're buggered, mate. I said this in English, too. It's probably self-evident which parts I'm speaking in French and which parts in English, but as a public service to the obvious-impaired I will occasionally point these parts out.

I have to go to Paris to speak to the bank in person.

You have your passport?

Yes, but no money for a plane ticket. Or a taxi or a car service or, for example, a sandwich.

I repeat: buggered. Up the junction.

Is it possible to borrow some money from you?

No, it is not possible.

But you know that I am rich.

I know that *I'm* rich. I don't know anything about you. I've heard these identity theft cases can go on for years.

I was going to lend him money. But I enjoyed toying with him, and we both knew that as a condition of lending him money I would make him help me find his brother and my sister.

I will go to the press, he said.

That's your play? You want the *New York Times* and *Le Monde* writing about how your brother stole your identity and locked you in an abandoned cannery near the East River?

No. But that is the truth.

Sounds like the plot of one of your own novels. All of France will be laughing at you.

All of France is already laughing at me. I don't care (*je m'en fous*). I want my life back.

I sat down on the bed and folded my arms in my lap. I was starting to enjoy myself.

Come with me to find my sister. Once we're sure she's safe, I will lend you whatever funds you require.

If you have so much money, why are you a translator?

Why are you a writer? If you *are* a writer.

I tell you I am H! *The* H!

Yeah, not good enough. I've no proof H can write.

I've sold thousands of books. I'm the most famous writer in France.

Which only proves that the French have terrible taste. A fact I already know, which is why I live here, where this is common knowledge about the French.

Fine, yes, OK. I agree to your terms. Having no other option. May I please have some money now?

57

If H1 were to mulct me for even twenty dollars, he'd give me the slip, and though I neither needed nor wanted him with me, I couldn't let him run away from the situation, because I wanted to run away from the situation, and when everybody runs away from the situation fascism happens, or the death of journalism, or pythons running wild in the Everglades. Anyway, he could help. I had a few ideas where to look for H2, but H1 knew his hotspots. Should the trail run cold in Cap Ferret, he could point me to the Swiss chalet outside Montreux. Or the apartment in Venice. Or, whatever, the houseboat on the River Cam or the mountain lair at Innsbruck. Wherever H2 was, I needed to go. I couldn't save my sister over the phone or by any other indirect means. Nor could A fend for herself. She never could before, and she certainly couldn't now after years of otiose living, her every whim satisfied by paid vassals.

My mother said that A said that I already had A's new phone number. Meaning: someone planted it on me. I searched through the papers and books on my desk. On the back of one of the notebook pages in the top folder was a red ink scrawl in a neat hand that was not mine. It was a British cellphone number. Which could easily have been planted while I was drugged and pinioned like a butterfly. Or during the I-don't-know-how-long it took to spirit me back to my apartment.

I painstakingly entered each of the numbers in the long form you have to use when dialling overseas, still, in the twenty-first century. The dial tone was British; there were three rings before a sleepy female voice answered.

V? said the voice.

A?

What's going on? Maman said you were in trouble.

There was the sound of her muffling the phone with her hand, talking to someone else. A lengthy stretch of fraught silence.

A? I said, after a while, making a wtf gesture to H1, who shrugged.

Hello, Vanessa. This is H2.

What are you doing with my sister?

She's here of her own free will. She can leave any time.

Put her back on the phone.

That is not possible. I had to give her an injection of a powerful sedative.

You rapey fucking bastard. I will rip your balls out with my teeth.

He sighed. So much spirit. Such a waste.

Where are you?

I cannot tell you where I am. I value too greatly my balls.

I hung up. I had an idea.

I have an idea, I said to H1.

I went to my laptop and logged into Apple Support. Looked for a number where I could call a human person.

Called. Waited on hold. While I was waiting I decided to make H1 and myself a Singani Sazerac.

2 OZ SINGANI 63

2 CUBES DEMERARA SUGAR

3 DASHES PEYCHAUD'S BITTERS

ABSINTHE

LEMON TWIST

RINSE ROCKS GLASS WITH ABSINTHE AND DISCARD EXCESS. BURN ABSINTHE FOR 10 SECONDS, THEN EXTINGUISH. STIR REMAINING INGREDIENTS OVER ICE IN A MIXING GLASS, THEN STRAIN INTO A ROCKS GLASS. SQUEEZE LEMON TWIST OVER DRINK AND GARNISH.

SAZERAC

Three hours and several of these delicious creations later, I was talking to an apparently human person who claimed to be endowed with the requisite authority.

My name is Angelique de Saxe, I said. Someone stole my phone. And I'm away from my computer so I can't use 'Find My iPhone' because I don't remember my iCloud username or password.

I know everything about A, because almost everything about A is the same as everything about me. I was taking a chance that H2 would be overconfident enough not to throw away A's real phone, whose number I still had in my contacts. I figured that the number I'd called was a burner acquired for single use. But if he'd kept her iPhone, and left it on – there would be good reasons for doing so if he wanted to keep up the illusion that she had not been kidnapped – I'd be able to track her to wherever they were.

The process of getting Apple Support to reset A's username and password is called social engineering by hackers. I know this because I once translated an Italian thriller about cybercrime that was so convincing I threw out my digital devices and rebooted my life with new, air-gapped devices, despite which I'm convinced everyone is tracking my every keystroke. There's a word for this new kind of paranoia, or there should be. Not that it matters. We know we're being watched and we keep playing with our toys. Maybe we like being watched.

H1 was drifting around my living room, gawking at the art on my walls.

What is this blurry photo? he asked.

Francesca Woodman. She killed herself in 1981.

Because she couldn't figure out how to focus her camera?

Threw herself out of this apartment. That's why I bought it.

The apartment or the photograph?

Both.

He didn't have anything smart to say after that. Or ever, but I'm not the type who keeps score.

I like the one with the swan, he said.

But that was in another country, and besides the wench is dead, I said, because I didn't want him to see my emotional response to the mention of my favourite photograph.

Check out the Charline von Heyl painting on the other wall, I said. More your speed, I should think.

He walked over to the painting.

Why do you say that? he said. It's hideous.

It's called *Bois-Tu De La Bière?* I said.

He stationed himself directly in front of the emphatically yellow canvas edged with spidery black scratches which spread and triangulated towards the middle.

It's still hideous.

Somehow, at length, my daft plan worked. I reset A's password. I logged into her account and tracked her phone.

What the hell, I said, as the map scrolled and then centred, a blue dot pulsing where her phone, and hopefully A, were situated.

H1 looked over my shoulder. Where is this?

Ever been to France? I said. Using my sarcastic voice. AKA my voice.

I never leave Paris, he said.

It's in the Alps. The fucking Alps.

58

H1 glowered on the couch. He was trying to out-stubborn me, but I cannot be out-stubborned. He stood no chance, and he knew it, hence the frowny sulk.

You're coming to the Alps, I said. It's your brother. It's my sister. I had my back to him as I fiddled with some settings on my mobile to enable, in advance, international use. I continued: You have an obligation.

I loathe cold weather, snow and heights, he said. The Alps to my knowledge feature these in abundance. I develop chilblains easily. Additionally, I have no obligation. I disown my brother. Half-brother.

I don't think you can disown a sibling, I said. You can disown a child, but not a sibling. In the strictest sense. Perhaps disavow is the word you want.

I disavow you.

Fine with me, I said. As a side note, you have no money, no credit cards and nowhere to stay. If you don't come with me, I'll throw you out in the street without a second thought.

That's how you disown someone, I thought with some satisfaction.

He pouted.

You are cruel, he said.

You're a cunt. On your bike, Mike.

He looked at me blankly.

C'est une expression anglaise. Ça veut dire on y va.

D'accord, he said, getting up from the couch. *Mais je ne suis pas 'Mike'.*

Grip a couple of bottles of Singani with your podgy paws, Mickey, I said.

This was just for the trip to the airport. I would need one bottle for myself to put up with H1 and one for H1 to pacify him. Or vice versa. It's possible that the events of the past few weeks are playing out on a loop as in *The Invention of Morel*, but I don't see the harm in adequately self-medicating myself and my travelling companion against the rigours of the peripatetic life on the one hand and the chance of discovering the secret horror of life on the other.

By the time we pulled up in our Uber at JFK, I was already sick of H1's incessant whingeing. He wanted to smoke. I refused. He wanted to make as if every time we went round a sharp curve that gravity was forcing his head across the seat and into my boobs. I pushed his head back so hard against the passenger window I thought it would break. His head and/or the window. Either would have been fine.

Even in first class, with the seats far enough apart that you can ignore a persistent boor, he was unbearable. If it's all persona, mumming, then it's an act that's overtaken whoever the real Not Michel Houellebecq is or was. If that's who he was or is, I quit. Except I can't quit, which sucks.

I was stuck in an aluminium bacillus lab with a leering, wheezing, wall-eyed homunculus. H1's presence on my current mission was an unfortunate side effect of the absurdity circumscribing that mission. His propinquity gnawed at my vitals even when – check that, *especially* when – like now, he was unconscious and snoring, his head against the reclined seat's headrest, lolling from side to side, mouth open, thick lips dribbling strings of drool down either side of his chin. Everything about H1 seemed designed by some malevolent deity to irritate me.

Lately I've noticed small things that didn't use to irritate me have grown, over time, into ogres of irritation that I cannot ignore. One of these is snoring. Another is drooling while snoring. But when I was growing up these phenomena fascinated rather than repelled me. I could watch my father sitting in his armchair for hours, ostensibly poring over the catalogue for some upcoming film festival, in reality dozing, head back, fine Gallic/Jewish nose elevated towards the ceiling, snoring his bloody head off like a bad actor in a cheap teleplay; I would poke him with utensils to see what effect this would have on the volume or timbre of his snores; I would play with the drool that ran down his face, twisting his spittle into curlicues of mucus that I would sometimes lick fondly, which, don't knock it until you've tried it. But sometime after coming down from Oxford and emigrating to New York I developed an intolerance for snoring, drooling and, worst of all, anyone talking to me or at me without my having invited or initiated the conversation. Your blandishments re my looks are neither welcome nor useful unless you're a fan of boots-up-the-ass, which you may be. As I have been informed by pop music, it takes all kinds.

It has ever been a hindrance to some and a blessing to others that the inbred egoism of the human race blinkers even the perceptive nature. The world revolves, we can agree. But secretly each believes that it revolves around them. Knowing this is a help to the salesperson and the diplomat, but no comfort to the distressed creature who convinces themselves that the machinery of the universe has uniquely conspired to obturate them in the hunt for happiness.

Here's a picture taken while drunk on airplane wine:

59

I nurtured some hope that as eight-hour plane flights with uncompanionable companions go, this one, thanks to some planning on my part, would not be among the worst I had endured. This was assuming we were not troubled by undue turbulence or unruly terrorists, which are the two most irksome of the many indignities of aviation today. I am an uneasy flyer, but not for the usual reasons. I'm not afraid of crashing, burning, dying. What it comes down to, my friends, as is so often the case re *moi*, is that I do not enjoy being caged for extended spans of time and/or space with other people. I don't believe that *l'enfer, c'est les autres*, either in the popular sense of those words or in the ontologically complex way Sartre meant those words to be understood, but as I hope I have made clear I am a selfish and judge-y misanthrope, so yeah, no, I don't like being in a plane. But when I do fly, I fly first class, so *les autres* aren't the issue so much as the inherent constrictions of flight. No getting round the fact that once the plane leaves the gate you cannot get off that plane until it docks at its terminus, and that's a prison *selon moi*. It is, I admit, a first-class prison, but a prison nonetheless.

Other kinds of travel (train, car, boat, hovercraft) feature other kinds of asperities, but it's only air travel where I'm prevented from using my AK: which is to say my hollowed-out copy of *Anna Karenina* wherein I've jammed a plastic bag of various illegally obtained prescription and street drugs. I've got opiates, muscle relaxants, tranquillisers, various forms of stimulants, beta blockers, psychedelics, sleeping pills, pure MDMA and some particularly potent hash. I keep two copies. One in my apartment in the East Village, another in a locker at CDG that I can pick up and re-deposit after clearing customs on arrival and before going through security on departure.

My AK has in the least dramatic way possible saved my life. Or made my life temporarily bearable, which amounts to the same thing. The day Thomas Early killed himself, for example. That whole week. I blotted the ripe-blue sun of my consciousness from the cotton-red welkin of my life with several dozen Cumulus Oxycontin (not all at once, but I do have a high tolerance), with the result that I remember nothing about the two weeks after he died. I did stuff. I ate. I talked to people on the phone. I wrote emails. I watched movies on my laptop. I may have done some work. On a short-term basis, opiates can be effective in focusing the brain on work. But I don't recommend addiction.

Specifically for air travel, however, I have additionally amassed a portable pharmacy of legally obtained prescriptions from my psychiatrist, Mother Sugar, for help with my floriferous bouquet of real physical and psychological issues. These prescriptions can come in handy even when I don't myself require their use. I've found that if you dissolve forty milligrams of zolpidem in a glass of red airplane wine, H1 will lose consciousness within twenty minutes of take-off and you won't have to talk to him until you land at Charles de Gaulle, and after waking he will be as fuzzy and pliant as a baffled sloth until you've bundled him in a cab to Gare de Lyon and onto the TGV. By the time his me-induced demi-coma had worn off, we were in Grenoble.

60

Secret Properties of the Triangle

Envy is the radix malorum in Dante and the common currency of mimetic desire in Girard. In French (check w V) it's commonly rendered as la jalousie which is also the name of a book by that nouveau roman guy she worships.

The epidemic of stress. Black Plague of the 21st century. She has no patience for his dream, his wisdom tooth, his fears about the church bells. She tells him to go get his jacket. Phone doesn't work. She's fed up. He's having a nervous breakdown. An alarm. Or is it a signal. Pull yourself together. What is it now? You can't be so sensitive. Can't you ever shut up? Military convoy. She apologizes. In car to ferry he says tomorrow it'll be four years. At bridge they buy fish. He watches her, overwhelmed with love. Car radio always broken. It's better not to know anything. I'm fed up with your escapism. I'm not going to argue with you. We're going to have fish for dinner. When you were talking to him I felt so in love with you. You were so beautiful! From a distance, right?

Theater of disintegration. They used to play music together.

The swans are emblematic of.

Wombed in sin darkness. Spouse and helpmate of Adam Kadmon: Heva, naked Eve. She had no navel. They clasped and sundered, did the coupler's will. In a Greek water closet he breathed his last: euthanasia. With bearded mitre and with crozier, stalled upon his throne, widower of a widowed see, with upstiffed omophorion, with clotted hinderparts.

Couldn't he fly a bit higher than that? Poor phoenix. In the park, nailed to the flowery froth of the sea-foamed night. Entailed on them indelible disgrace. Entail him and his heirs unto the crown. All existence is self-conscious.

There have been (at least) five mass extinction events in the fossil record. Two of the largest (the Ordovician/Silurian, c. 470 million years ago) and the Triassic (c. 230 million years ago) were ANOXIC EVENTS (basically large-scale removal of oxygen from atmosphere) accompanied by Ice Ages, and began under much the same conditions we have (re)created through our own rapacious avidity: an excess of CO_2 and other green-house gases in the atmosphere, nutrient drain-off into oceans, consequent warming of ocean (which is essentially a huge heat sink). In past anoxic events, this has triggered enormous algae/plankton blooms that eat carbon dioxide and 1) draw off huge amounts of oxygen, almost half current amounts, suffocating most animal life, marine and terrestrial and 2) drastically lower ocean and thus global temperatures to Ice Age levels.

Typically what first happens in these events is that environmental AND oceanic greenhouse gas concentrations rise above sustainable levels (however defined), prompting superblooms of phytoplankton in the oceans. The reason this draws off rather than produces more O_2: during daylight hours, phytoplankton do produce oxygen as a byproduct of photosynthesis, but that oxygen is dissolved into the ocean, and at night, the density of the superblooms reduces the dissolved oxygen through respiration.

It's important to note that phytoplankton photosynthesis has regulated the atmospheric CO_2/O_2 level since the Precambrian era 4.6 billion–540 million years ago (basically since the Earth first formed). When that process is interfered with—in the past this has occurred via volcanic eruptions, tectonic disturbances resulting in what's called a methane burp, and collisions with asteroids—you get radical changes to the ecological balance and consequently mass extinctions.

Photosynthesis in terrestrial plants accounts for a relatively small percentage (less than 20%) of the CO_2/O_2 balance. Interestingly, it's not insects (i.e. cockroaches) that have survived every prior mass extinction event, but plants. Plants always survive.

In every prior case this process took thousands/millions of years to complete. Because the process of global warming in this case has been so accelerated, it's reasonable to predict a planetary defense reaction (which is actually what happened in these previous anoxic extinction events) that's much faster; i.e. to posit that human-driven climate change in the form of ever-increasing CO_2 levels and nitrogen runoff from fertilizers on an industrial, heretofore unseen scale, in addition to methane emissions both from livestock and from melting Arctic permafrost, and on and on, might result in a greatly accelerated process.

61

I'm tempted to write something vapid about the illegibility of even the people closest to you, particularly in the case of a person as interiorly shut as Thomas, which is a trait I understand to be common among serious writers and weightlifters. I'm grateful to him for slipping his notebook among my papers, so that I might derive a deeper awareness of his essential sadness. It's awful to think that the person sleeping next to you is gripped by fears you neither know nor recognise, and that even if you knew and recognised his fears you couldn't help. Fear is individual. It's part of the self-built self. None of us is free from fear, but for the most part this is evolution's residue, squatting in our lizard brain, uncontrollable and almost always unhelpful.

The existential dread from which Thomas suffered was man-made. Literally artificial. Fiat Lux didn't title her best book *Artificial Light* on a whim. The whole of that unwieldy masterpiece was devoted to the idea that not just fear but the better part of consciousness is *constructed*; handmade by elves. Artifice lies at art's heart and is necessary to its design; but, like everything with three or thirteen dimensions, artifice has a B-side. Art's shadow, the self, shrouds a killer instinct that too often succeeds. We do not exist except via an act of artifice, and we cannot unexist except via an act of deconstruction from which the bravest quail. Being is a joke, but it's the best joke ever. Not even Dante's unfunny *Comedy* can gainsay that.

The key attribute of any creative effort is that it has no motive. You might think you have a motive, like my Tom, but you're acting out a passion play that was out of date before the painted Palaeolithic bulls on the walls of Lascaux were dry. What threw Thomas was the inexpressibility of things-beyond-thought. When you've breached the bounding line of words, or what words can do, the only thing left is to shut up in some final way.

Too many of us are afflicted with hope to close every trap-door to the possible. Here's the sitch: there is no plan; we're not in this together: exactly the opposite. You will die alone. It might happen today. It might already have happened, but you were too busy gaping at your phone to notice, waiting for a notification from some higher force, in the clouds or in the Cloud, that came too late, and now it's too late.

It was always gonna be too late. It was too late for Thomas, it's too late for me, and it's transparently too late for you, my hypothetical reader, my likeness, my bitch twin sister.

62

To my mild surprise, H1 was pleased to find himself in Grenoble. In the first place, it wasn't as he'd feared some dingy village in the Alps. In the second place, I'd put us up in the Grand Hôtel, the nearest to a five-star hotel in the city. Because it was almost Christmas, the hotel was unpeopled, and I was able to get us suites next to each other for far less than the going rate.

In the third place, H1 liked Grenoble. I did, too. It's a more colourful city than Paris, in a literal sense — the buildings are painted more colourfully — though nobody's going to confuse it with Lisbon. It's ringed by mountains which on a clear day you can see in detail, and it's compact and easily walkable. One can find several tolerable restaurants, and most importantly for H1's mental well-being, the hotel was directly across from a Monoprix, the not-even-Whole Foods of France. He is besotted with that place. God knows why, or God doesn't know why, God shrugs and rolls her eyes whenever H1 strolls through the automatic doors and down to the basement level where they keep the food-like items, including the bags of two dozen individually wrapped madeleines that H1 gorged on by the fistful. I would not like to be H1's intestinal tract.

There's probably no more polluted place on earth outside Chernobyl, and Chernobyl has the advantage of depopulation and disuse. While you could make the argument that H1's intestinal tract was underpopulated, it was not depopulated, and while it was likewise seldom used, it was often abused, and that is worse.

Other items found at the bottom of H1's plastic-handled shopping cart: a jar of olive tapenade, several litres of different hybrid flavours of Tropicana juice (apple-lychee his favourite, peach-mango his second favourite), bogus tiramisu in plastic bowls, four to a pack, several varieties of prepackaged chicken sandwich, and pasta salad. The pasta salad was a concession to his idea of my idea of healthy food, though I did not care what garbage he shovelled into his pie-hole and would certainly not have picked pre-processed pasta salad as an alternative poison.

The dietary item we agreed on was alcohol; that it should be good; that it should be plentiful. The Grenoble-Centre Monoprix had a decent wine selection and did not overcharge as much as, say, Nicolas, or the market stall in the centre of town which sold me a 2004 Pauillac for forty euros that turned out to be corked. We bought cases of Burgundy and Bordeaux and a sizable quantity of AOC cheeses and fresh bread. These last were for me, along with some decent foie gras and wild boar sausage. The food was richer than my digestion was prepared to handle, but after a three-day transition period I adjusted well enough.

On the fourth day, I went so far as to take a shower, which, I know, look out world. I was admiring my naked body in the mirror in the bathroom when H1 knocked on the front door of my suite.

Hold on, I shouted towards the door. I'm rather in the state of Manet's *Olympia*.

What?

Or Goya's *La maja desnuda*.

What?

Titian's *Venus*, then.

What?

I'm bloody naked, hang on a sec, will you? God, the culture on this world-class ass. I grabbed one of the hotel's plush monogrammed robes and threw it over my magnificent self. Had he shown a groat's worth of wit, I might have favoured him with a glimpse of my boobs.

Here is a picture of the cathedral at Chartres:

63

The snow-shrouded peaks clumped around Grenoble are not the world. The world is the totality of facts, not things. *Wovon man nicht sprechen kann, darüber muss man schweigen.* Easy to say, you see, less easy for others to rappel (or ascend). Mind the words! Sunlight has different qualities at different times of day. These are apparent and non-apparent, appearing and non-appearing. You feel sunlight but you don't *feel* the sunlight, because the air is so cold the sun can't help you. The sun's like, *Sorry, pal, doing my best, but you're on your own.*

It's best to learn lessons like this from the sun. You're never going to listen to your parents, and God's a bore, but the sun's been there for you every day of your life, and never in a hectoring or insistent way. You can always get away from the sun if you want (I often do; not a sun fan) by crossing the street. The sun is the opposite of H1, who, like the moon, is a cold dead rock with no atmosphere. Also, he only wakes up at night.

I was patient with him for the first several days of our sojourn in Grenoble. While I did the investigative groundwork, he holed up in the hotel drinking and smoking (on the balcony, complaining every minute about the cold and the damp, as if the cold and the damp aren't the elements from which he's fashioned) and occasionally eating. Nothing more fun than coming back from a long day of tracking down leads and/or weapons to find H1 leaning on the wrought-iron balcony railing silhouetted in a musing and decorous wraith of smoke by the setting sun, cigarette in one hand, glass of Beaujolais in the other.

I didn't care. I was in an OK mood because I had managed to geolocate my sister and H2 in or near a system of caves about an hour outside the city that lay in a valley surrounded by the chemical factories that along with ski and snowboard vacationers have ruined the French Alps. It remained but to convince H1 that what I planned to do next a) required his help and b) was the right way to go. This did not prove to be easy, but I did not expect it to prove easy, and in this I was proved right, which is better than easy.

We went downstairs to a café near the hotel. I had an espresso, he had a glass of Côtes du Rhône. We sat outside on the gas-lamp-heated *terrasse* so that he could smoke. He was bundled up as if he were going skiing on Mount Helicon during a blizzard. I wore a blue sweater.

During the subsequent discussion I felt like Levin in a non-hollowed-out copy of *Anna Karenina* trying to explain his ideas for agrarian reform to his bailiff. H1 was gloomily dismissive when I put forward my plans.

You do not know anymore how things work in France, he told me, as though in the few years since I lived here the nation had somehow unrecognisably transformed.

I think I do, I said, which I admit is weak, ripostely speaking.

It is impossible.

This is a bad translation. If I were translating dialogue in an actual book I'd be ashamed to put 'It is impossible' for *C'est impossible*, but I'm transcribing from notes I made on a hotel pad with a hotel pen hours after the fact, and as I'm no longer sure that I will have time to write down everything that happened or will happen in a manner befitting my stylistic pretensions, I'm not letting the small stuff sweat through my large-pored prose.

I resisted the temptation to reply, *No, you're impossible,* and instead confined myself to an eye-roll of disgust at his unwarranted miserabilism.

We know where H2 is holding my sister, I said, and he's probably there as well. We cannot risk the police. You know this guy – your brother – better than I do, but we can both agree he's not *compos mentis* and maybe never has been. The first sign of cops, he'll start shooting. Maybe we'll get lucky and he'll start with himself, but more likely he'll hit you, or me, or her, or, worse yet, some innocent passerby.

No one is innocent.

Whatever. The cops are a non-starter. If you have any sense of decency – Christ, never mind, look who I'm talking to.

Do not confuse my persona with my person. That's what the press does. Frankly I don't care, but still.

I don't care about your persona or your person. You're here because I saved your ass, and you're going to help me because you owe me. This was not the full truth, as I had in no real sense saved H1's ass, but I thought if I put my case forcefully he wouldn't notice the flaw in my logic.

If we go in as you suggest, the gendarmes will be on top of us in twenty seconds. This is a country held fast by hoops of fear, you understand me? The slightest breath of terror is met by the full force of the state.

That's possibly the most banal thing you've ever said.

Nevertheless.

I'm done discussing this. We will drive to the cave and you will talk your brother into releasing my sister. What happens after that, to you or to anyone else, does not concern me.

I will be free after this.

You're already free. It's just that if you don't do what I say I'll fucking kill you. But you could certainly *choose* not to do what I say.

What happens if I can't convince my brother?

Plan B involves the automatic rifles, 9 mm handguns and grenades I bought off a drug gang early this morning.

I do not like Plan B.

Nobody likes Plan B. That's why it's called Plan B.

This, too, is banal.

Go fuck yourself in the fucking ass with a fuck pen – that you bought from the fuck store.

I stood and jarred the table, spilling his glass of wine all over my jeans.

He almost smiled.

64

The breadcrumbs Thomas left me are not helping me, if that was his intent, follow his orbit of thought. The more I learn about him through his writing, the more he recedes in my consciousness, becomes formless, ambiguous. Though he was never exactly solid when alive, he's become vaporous in death. The picture I hold of him in my mind has begun to waver and scatter like light through a glass of water. Some of that is to be expected: when the object of perception disappears from regular view, your brain can only reconstruct parts of it, and only against the background of a particular table in a particular room, at a particular time of day. Some memories require context to make sense, do not exist in the unreal space of a portrait or a picture. I've begun to grasp that words do not help provide that context. They serve but to jumble the lines.

I picked up H1 from in front of the hotel in a rented black Peugeot 508. I'd have preferred a Mercedes E-Class, but you can't always rent what you want. We drove through the centre of town along typically twisty and narrow streets, medieval planning gone to seed, or to plan, out of the city and north towards the Chartreuse mountains. We were headed to the

Dent de Crolles, where according to my information H2 and my sister had gone to ground somewhere in the extensive system of subterranean caverns.

It was a straight shot east on the A41, past the hypermarket opposite the University of Grenoble and up along the Isère river past the old Aerodrome du Versoud, where nothing bad has happened, turning north at the D30. You can see the Massif de la Chartreuse as soon as you leave the city, but the Dent de Crolles is two thousand metres up, and you have to take that two thousand metres by long, meandering roads that are as narrow as those in Grenoble centre-ville but far more dangerous, especially at this time of year, when the signs warning of *verglas* round every bend have to be taken seriously.

We were stopping, though H1 didn't yet know it, at the Restaurant Le Funiculaire in Saint-Hilaire, which, as the name suggests, sits at the entrance to the funicular that would ferry us down to the Grésivaudan valley, a dizzying descent that I expected would evoke a squall from my fellow traveller. I knew, however, that if you gave H1 good food and enough alcohol, he would do almost any fool thing, including taking a funicular a thousand or so metres down to a valley where, if all went according to my fiddly plan, we would find H2 and my sister. In September, the restaurant hosts something called the Coupe Icare, which (so the story goes) is the biggest assemblage in the world of what is charmingly called in French *les adeptes du vol libre*, better known to you and me as barmy people who parasail down from the Massif de la Chartreuse to the Grésivaudan valley. I admit that, had it not been for the season, I might have been tempted to give it a go.

But I'm a practical girl. No way was I going to be able to get H1 down the mountain in anything other than a precipitous and ancient train, and even that would be a trial.

The important point was that I remembered to bring the duffel bag full of weapons.

65

Pasted into Thomas Early's notebook on laser-printed paper in a minuscule font was the following, which I guess to be a rough draft of the suicide note he never got to leave me:

The luster of the present hour is always borrowed from the background of possibilities it goes with. William James

That the effective world of the individual according to W. James in his *Varietals* is practically real. Tolstoy's anhedonia. What M. Yourcenar calls the sinuosity characteristic of his literary game when discussing Mann, in whom she invests too much of her particular genius for analysis. He is not worthy of your brain, Marguerite, you want to shout at the black and tan pages of her second-best book.

The winnowing basket as representation of Dionysus. Among the Tanala people of Madagascar almost all children born in the unlucky month of Faosa are buried alive in the forest (J-L-G Frazer, *Spirit(s) of the Corn and of the Wilde*, Vol. 1, p. 666). Riz-pain-sel in the work of Huysmans means something other than food, just as corn does not mean corn in Frazer, when he is talking of corn. He does not mean maize. He does not mean MON 810. Who is walking away from Molloy, what breed of dog does he nuzzle, what is he smoking? He hears the angelus and recalls the incarnation. That is so you.

I put a letter in the box for the mail lady to take away later. The letter contains instructions to my family that are not instructions, more like requests as to how I would like my obsequies to be handled when I die.

There is a madman in an asylum in Paris who appears perfectly lucid to me. The letter he writes to his doctor complaining of bad insomnia and omnipresent fear such that he wishes for nothing so much as he wishes for death, or (and this is perhaps what makes him mad?) never to have been born. If you can compose such a letter even in the grip of a terrible fear I don't think you're hopeless. I would need to know more about the circumstances. Was the letter written of the writer's volition or at the request of someone else or as a form of therapy? (Roubinovitch et Toulouse: *La Mélancolie*, 1897, p. 170, abridged.) The letter is almost intolerably sad. I say raved, for I can write no otherwise. That is poetry.

I was once accused of writing poetry, but I managed to dodge the charge by proving that I had no talent. In the courts you can prove anything if you have convictions. The hardest part about proving that you have no talent is that people are so encouraging. Many believe that everyone has talent, or a talent, that it lies dormant and awaits discovery. That may be true in a plurality but is not true in me. One obdurate admirer insisted that since I did not have talent

I must have genius, because in her view genius was an unobstructed view of the self, and my recognition of my lack of talent was in itself the rarest talent. I mocked her, I called her Socrates, which was unkind (I am also unkind), but I meant to say that she was using sophistry, which is what Socrates did not do and exposed at regularly spaced intervals. Even my insults are talentless.

The regrets that sting the most involve disappointing other people. One regrets hurting people, in any sense of the word (people), but letting someone down is the pits. In that sense, were we cataloging my bountiful faults, my unerring instinct for incurring disappointment in others, while not as interesting as my inability to show up late for any appointment, would either place or show.

That I suffer from competence may well be my greatest fear. That I am good at something. That I've learned enough to be good. Please dear God, if you exist, save us from pedagogy. From competence, confidence, skill, and craft. From the stunting elements of style, the rudiments, the mastery of fundamentals. Give us instead the wild hot breath of uncomfortable lies poorly told but sung, swung, or slung down the gas line to the engine. Give us music.

[V of course you understand the above para as parody. Even in death I smile, and smiling bend to kiss your tulips. We live in a post-taste world, and it's killing me.]

Sume, lege, were the words Augustine heard in the garden, and he did take and he did read, opening his Bible at random and finding a passage that seemed directly to address him. I don't doubt the truth of his account, but how different is this from anyone who picks up the horoscope section of the newspaper, back when there were newspapers, and finds in his daily forecast an analogue to everything that has happened or will happen or is happening? The truth is not what you see but what you want to see. The truth is an act of volition rather than perception.

Goodbye Vanessa. Goodbye, goodbye, goodbye.

66

Gérard de Nerval used to walk a lobster on a bright blue ribbon-leash round the Palais-Royal. This according to Théophile Gautier. Who may have been making a point or relating a point that Nerval was making about the arbitrary nature of what kinds of animals we humans choose to recognise as pets, or what behaviour we choose to regard as normal in human beings. In other words, Gérard de Nerval may well never have walked a lobster on a bright blue ribbon-leash round the Palais-Royal. But I've heard and accepted as true all my life the story that he did. It's no use telling me that it doesn't matter whether or not he did, because that isn't or wasn't the point of Gautier's anecdote. I don't care about the point of Gautier's anecdote. It is a matter of life or death to me, on the other hand, whether or not a lobster was walked on a bright blue ribbon-leash by Gérard de Nerval round the Palais-Royal.

My opinion, Thomas Early: if you accept one thing as true-in-spirit rather than true-in-fact, then everything and nothing is true-in-fact, and that's when problems of more than a purely epistemological nature arise. Though my subscription copies of the *New York Review of Books* and the *New Yorker* and the *Paris Review* and *Harper's* et al. continue to pile up unread on my reclaimed Russian oak coffee table, I have been for some time aware of the term post-truth, which has been applied with abandon or abandoned with application, one of these, to any perceived emanation of the spirit of our times. This bothers me. To a point I agree with you, my dead lover, I don't think there are individual truths that apply only to an individual's subjectively lived experience. These are more properly called perspectives, and are infinitely valuable as such, but should not be confused with truths, which are surely collated from the sum of subjective perspectives and not produced by them. Or owned by any individual or group of human beings. Otherwise truths would multiply like fruit flies, and live as briefly and pointlessly. An ontology that allowed for multiplicative truths would end up looking bloated and misshapen, something like one of the varieties of anthroposophical thought promoted by Rudolf Steiner in the early twentieth century. I admit that this resulted in some great art and significantly weird architecture, notably the first and second Goetheanums at Dornach, but if you've read any of his books you can't help but feel that the poor man was under the influence of a series of potent delusions, any one of which extended to its logical conclusion would undercut the others.

I'm not opposed to the Esoteric traditions in Western or Eastern or Middle Earth thought but I do think these traditions need to be situated properly in the context of a broader trend towards individualist humanism that has proved no less a dead end than Marxism. Bits and bobs of *veritas* float in every religious bromide but do not in themselves add up to much. If you're looking, as I have been looking and still am looking, for an all-encompassing story in which to fold the many-coloured cloth of existenz, look to history. As I have looked to history. *Because I am convinced that human history has a meaning; and that meaning is terrifying. It has to do with the primacy of violence in human relations.*

We live in a time when the opiate of the masses is actually opiates, when our best hope to avoid a climacteric climate catastrophe is a pandemic that wipes out two-thirds of humanity. Thomas used to call the general shape of things World Fever, and you could say that in the end he was the first victim of his own made-up disease. Please bear in mind that Thomas was writing about World Fever years before World Fever actually became a thing, in other words when it was still cool. As with Hilma af Klimt, neither he nor I could stand when things we had adopted as private and sacred suddenly exploded into worldwide celebrity. But I don't think the Actual Pandemic was the reason Thomas jumped to his death outside the same building where Francesca Woodman jumped to her death in 1981. I don't think Thomas's leap of unfaith was *unrelated* to Francesca's leap, either, and the result was the same. Thomas prattling about a *post-taste world* was not even original, it was an idea he ripped off from the lead girl in his favourite band Death Hags. I accept the proposition that we live in a post-taste world, and find the idea as depressing as anyone, but I'm not going to off myself over it, precisely because if you do accept the proposition, nothing matters, and if nothing matters, why bother with self-harm?

Everyone who commits suicide does so for a reason that makes sense to them in that instant, and if that instant passes, the result becomes a different result, a non-event that goes unrecorded in the annals of stuff that happened. Something did happen, but in the negative, which is to say it happened by not happening.

We don't have an effective way of recording these non-things, because by their nature they are elusive of discovery. Cicero's *Dream of Scipio* (*Somnium Scipionis*) would not have survived if Macrobius had not much later written a commentary on it, excerpting large portions, and even then his commentary became popular and the text was copied many times, introducing misconstructions and corruptions, so that no one knows what the true text of the *Dream of Scipio* looked like when Cicero wrote it, or what it means, except as reflected or refracted in derivative works like Dante's *Divine Comedy* or Chaucer's *Parliament of Birds*.

I'm not going to be Thomas's Macrobius, and if that was his intent in leaving me his notebook he will be looking on from Scipio's dream of the afterlife in dour disappointment.

67

It proved easier than I thought to get the Great Exigent H1 into the funicular. This is partly because he got tanked on Chartreuse at the restaurant, out of some ironic sense of place — I'll wait while you google Chartreuse, so you can read up about the monks, and the process by which they transform flowers into ichor, and so my lungs can get used to the thin air — and partly because he was in raptures about the contraption on first sight. You never know what's going to catch his good eye.

You probably came across *The Charterhouse of Parma* while you were searching. Stendhal was from Grenoble. His charterhouse had nothing to do with the Chartreuse that greened H1's gullet, except maybe in some oblique Anxiety of Influence way. I prefer génépi, but it's hard to get the real item even in the Alps where the flowers are native, albeit endangered.

The génépi flower with which one makes the génépi liqueur has a delicate, subtle scent that I would not have been able to identify or detect when I was a smoker. But I stopped smoking about five years ago, not long after I upped sticks to New York. Everything became clearer when I quit, but I quit on a whim. I wasn't worried about my health — I don't care about my health. Caring about your health is for stock-brokers. While I would rather talk to a stockbroker than a writer (a stockbroker has lived, and possibly knows about wine), I despise stockbrokers and have knowingly slept with one, once. And that was a hate-fuck. Stockbrokers care about their health, and are more likely to get annual physicals, visit the chiropractor regularly, practise mindfulness meditation and try to eat a healthy diet. Some stockbrokers go in for biohacking, like microdosing LSD or putting butter in their coffee or drinking an elixir refined from Finnish mushrooms. I don't do that – drugs are only any good when abused, and the point of taking a dietary supplement or a vitamin escapes me – but I no longer smoke. And that's when things got clearer. Especially my senses of smell and taste.

The funicular was painted a dull pea green, and its bolts were uniformly rusting, but it managed to creak and sway us from Point A to Point B, and while H2 burped and farted and mewled in unmixed awe, I stared uninflected out of the misted windows at the Alpine landscape. Landscapes do not evoke deep feeling in me, but I do revel in mountains. Anything montane or *montagneux*. Their prodigious unin-habited heights call to me, and I recapitulate. That's the main thing: no or few people.

    We got out at Point B with a young Swedish couple (pos-sibly Carl Linnaeus and his wife Sara looking for génépi in an alternate timeline) and a few drunk locals.

68

The Swedes went their way, the locals another, and we went ours. Or I went mine and H1 followed, burping and farting and mewling, though I was the one carrying the impedimenta and he only had to carry himself, upright, or upleft. Stop whingeing before I shove one of these semi-automatic rifles up your *cul* and *pule* the trigger, ran the course of my thoughts. You see what his incessant complaints have done to my ability to make coherent puns? He ruins everything, does H.

The cold was aqueous in its intensity. The air you drew into your lungs was like sludge, a compound of chemical factory effluvia and humidity and bad faith, and still you were supposed to trudge over the frozen ground, with its patina of snow-bits wheeling round your feet and occasionally up into the air and round your head, carrying on your shoulders a duffel bag filled with heavy guns and other weapons. And you did that. Or rather I did that. Uncomplaining. Unlike H1, whose default mode — I should know, I reset him enough times — was complaint, who was himself less a man than a compilation of complaints, and who nonetheless, I will give him this, followed me wherever I went, up steep hills and down narrow valley passes until we arrived at the snow-dusted couloir I had marked on my phone's GPS map with a digital X, punctuated on our arrival by an actual X, or ibex, who bounded away in fright, revealing a diminutive metal door in the side of the facing limestone cliff.

I'd expected the door, or a door, and because I was unsure what type of door and consequently lock I'd be dealing with, I'd brought a full set of lock-picking tools. I had not expected a door with no lock at all. But I could find no sign of one in the accepted sense of the word. The door was just a slab of smooth gunmetal grey slotted into the limestone. There was no visible hinge or handle. The sole ornament was an upside-down triangle with an eye in the middle, and in the centre of the eye a glass pupil that I presumed was a security device, activated by retinal scan or remote control. A sudden thought occurred to me, as is ever the wont of sudden thoughts.

I rummaged through my rucksack until I found and abstracted the credit card-sized device that H2 had given to me at his summer house in Cap Ferret, supposedly the key to my hotel room, but when I checked in I was given a different, old-fashioned key. There was a reason I'd never thrown out the high-tech key. That reason was that I liked the way it looked; I had no premonition of future utility, but still.

I pointed the device at the eye on the door and clicked it. A panel slid out of the door, flipping over to reveal a glassy pad that instructed me to put [my] right palm on the scanner, which scanner I assumed was the pad itself.

Here comes everyone, I said out loud. I knew, or suspected, that when I put my hand on the scanner the door would slide open, which it did, with a sonorous rumble, metal dragging over rock. The reason I knew or suspected that my handprint would work was that I knew or suspected that A's handprint would work and my handprint, though not identical, would, I reasoned or supposed, be close enough for horseshoes and hand grenades and first-gen handprint scanners. I shoved H1 through the door, threw the duffel bag after him, and quickly stepped inside. As soon as I did, the door slid shut behind us with the same sonorous rumble, closing with a satisfying *thunk*.

We were in a long tunnel that had been carved out of the rock, braced by two-by-fours along the sides and roof. A strip of white LED lights gemmed the way as far as we could see ahead. I didn't know whether these were always kept on or whether we'd triggered them by opening the door. Either way, I was going in on the assumption that our arrival had been announced. I took an automatic rifle out of the bag and racked it, hung a couple of grenades (one flash, one real) from my belt loops and shouldered the bag.

Let's go, I said to H1, who was sitting cross-legged on the ground, shivering as he watched me arm myself.

I'm not going anywhere, H1 said, predictably. I didn't want him with me, but I might need him nonetheless.

I don't want you with me, I said, but I might need you nonetheless. Off your butt. Follow me. Try not to die like a dog.

I stole that last line from Sir Ralph Richardson's instruction to Malcolm McDowell in O, Lucky Man!, fyi.

Nice, he said. He got up, groaning with the effort, whimpering about my bossy bitchiness, and followed unsteadily behind me towards the end of the tunnel.

For a good few minutes what lay ahead of us was nothing. The work on the tunnel looked recent, and well done. Stray clods of dirt would occasionally pelt us if we juddered the beams with my bag or our legs. H1 grunted and panted and made clear that he was putting in a heroic effort just by continuing to exist.

We continued down the tunnel until several people speaking in multicoloured voices made themselves plain round a curve in the brown rock. I motioned to H1 to stop, but he had already stopped. He was never not stopping.

Here is a picture of a swan:

The voices appeared to come from a larger space, and the light grew stronger closer to the noise. My guess: a cave. Good guess, Vanessa! Bet you're a whiz at quizzes. (I am.)

Cave coming up on the left, I said to H1, who did not appear to hear.

I signalled to him to stop.

You stay, I said. I'll check it out.

His head made a motion I chose to interpret as a nod.

I inchwormed to the mouth of the cave. No one stood guard, and I was able to lean forward enough to see that the ceiling was indiscernibly high. The light was from a blazing firepit, augmented by a grab bag of candles and a couple of strings of fairy lights. I saw the backs of a few people, seated, some of whom were wearing yellow safety vests. Which hoisted a corresponding yellow flag in my mind: *gilets jaunes*! If we'd stumbled onto those rapscallions we could expect unpleasantness. The *gilets jaunes*, named after the safety vests that French law requires all drivers to have in the car, began as a protest against a well-meant but ill-conceived petrol tax, but transformed quickly into a loosely organised peri-urban (because rural France barely exists anymore), anti-government, populist/nativist movement that had stopped making sense long ago but continued to agitate, scheme and complain for economic justice in the widest, vaguest, most frangible and least practical sense. The yellow jackets had no plan, no programme, stood for nothing, mistrusted politics and the political process, and as such were easily manipulated by conspiracy theorists, Russian bots and tricksy politicos. They had no sting, was my joke, but they did sting, which is why my joke wasn't funny.

At that second, as I considered my bad joke, I heard a woman laugh, and recognised that woman as my bitch twin sister.

Blinded by spleen, I wheeled into the cave and shouted at A. It was the laughter: not nervous laughter; not polite laughter; but full-throated laughter of the kind I have myself unleashed countless times and could probably forge if you had a gun to my head. I didn't believe A had a gun to her head.

I was wrong. H held a combat Mauser to her left temple. He barked sarcastically when he saw me. That shut me up quick; but not H2. He was expecting me; he'd been waiting for me; and my appearance did not discompose him in the least. An efflux of words issued from his mush, explaining who I was to the assembled yellow jackets, most of whom weren't, *stricto sensu*, yellow jackets, as they did not wear yellow jackets or vests. That distinction is probably too nice for the situation. He told them I was a daughter of privilege who unlike my twin had not bunged in with the cause the hour it was announced, that I was an empty-headed slut who thought only about her own material needs and pleasure. I was waiting for factitious insults, but I guess he figured a strictly accurate description of my character was enough to get everyone nettled.

Certainly I was nettled. Vexed, even. Not by his comments, which, as I say, were more descriptive than deprecating. I was vexed by the situation. But I wasn't confused. My senses were, so I thought, clear. Though the cave was lighted, you wouldn't call it well lit. The fire in the centre threw shadows against the walls. Now that I was inside I still couldn't see how high the cave went, because it disappeared into blackness some twenty metres from where I stood, but I could make out clusters of stalactites at varying heights. Around me were maybe two or three dozen men and women sitting on filthy mats and blankets or on the dirt of the cave floor itself, which was also studded with glittering rocks and towards the edges stalagmites that may have been coated in bat shit or layers of mineral deposit. My point is they glistened.

It was a potentially disorienting scene, but I did not, as I say, feel disoriented. My sister looked in good shape, considering, wearing a sprigged voile dress, blue-green shoes, and a necklace, with a fetching chocolate-brown surtout draped over her shoulders against the cold. Her left shoe was missing. She looked more bored than scared, and more annoyed than anything else. It was immediately apparent that she was not here under her own steam, that she had been tricked or coerced by H2. Her laugh – the inciting incident of my precipitous appearance – was clearly, in retrospect, contemptuous, judging not just from context but from the sneer she now directed at H2 as he spoke about me.

I was counting the seconds until H1 showed his repulsive wall-eyed face in the cave, unless – and I did not discount the notion – he was too cowardly to shift from the spot where I left him. As much as I wanted to see the look on

H2's face when confronted with his pseudo-doppelganger, I was more interested in extricating myself and A from the cave alive.

Could have sworn at that moment that I started hearing the noise of street traffic.

71

You may recall that I explained to H2 at some earlier point about my lack of any special connection with my bitch twin sister. It's not true, what I told him. We do have a connection. Nothing you couldn't dismiss as coincidence if you'd a mind to, but there were times, e.g., when we'd both be thinking the same thought and it wasn't an obvious thought and we'd look at each other and I knew, in that way that you can just know, that A was thinking the same thought. In those instances, we'd smile at each other.

When we were ten or eleven, under the influence of *L'Étranger* or something equally dopey, we used to torment the *bouquinistes* deployed along the Seine. We would dress identically and pop up now on one side, now on the other, of a given stall, asking snide questions like, Do you have a first edition of *As I Lay Dying*? Or any other book neither of us had an interest in acquiring. The one of us not appointed to ask the snide question would sneak behind the bookseller and pocket the book we wanted. We never agreed beforehand what books we wanted, and we would go down the row of *bouquinistes* as quickly and efficiently as possible, hitting every one. You couldn't do this every day, but once or twice a month was sufficient to sate our criminal impulses. We didn't need to steal books, we could buy whatever we wished, but maybe you need to sit down and have a serious talk with Colin Wilson, because it was his fault. Yes, I know he's dead.

My point in relating this spellbinding anecdote – picture us in our matching yellow dresses with white polka dots, our hair in pigtails, our cute patent-leather buckled shoes; now erase that imaginary image from your minds because we never dressed like that or wore our hair in pigtails – is that when we got home to examine our respective hauls, we had inevitably and always picked the same books. It was like a magic trick, but one that was being played on us by an unkind practitioner of the trade. I'd steal a cheap edition of *Voyage au bout de la nuit* (I was eleven years old, don't judge), and there on the thickly piled dark Persian carpet would be the same edition of the same book. Not exactly the same book, mind, that would be impossible, and maybe the condition was slightly different, mine with foxed pages, hers with some spotting, mine might be a second printing or hers a tenth, but nonetheless. However obscure or, conversely, popular our choices, we could never, somehow, unsync ourselves.

The years and physical distance had done that job for us; but had not sundered the link wholly, because A was smiling at me and I was smiling at her, and I knew what she was thinking, and she knew that I knew. What happened next was shocking but not surprising: A, in one abrupt and agile motion, turned towards H2, twisted his wrist, grabbed the gun from his hand, and shot him in the head.

In the tick before this happened, we both knew that it was the thing to do.

Ta gueule, I muttered, under my breath, as H2 slumped over, dead in an instant.

I should mention a couple of other points, to clear up any confusion you may be experiencing. I don't hate my bitch twin sister. I don't think she stole my life. I shouldn't call her my bitch twin sister but just my sister, my best friend, my light, my life. And one other thing.

She doesn't exist.

72

H1 came huffing into the cave, slinging the duffel bag before him. He looked at H2 slumped on the ground with a bullet in his head and raised an eyebrow.

You shot me, he said.

No, Angelica shot H2, I said.

No, you shot me. There is no Angelica. There is no H2. Your brother—

I don't have a brother. You don't have a sister. You brought me into an uninhabited cave deep in the Alps.

I don't— What do you mean you don't have a brother?

Violet—

My name is Vanessa.

I told you what would happen if there was gunfire. I told you that the gendarmes are on high alert. You hear that?

In the distance, faintly but distinctly, I heard sirens. Unaccountably, I also heard again the sound of street traffic. Blaring horns, squawking brakes. And a sudden gust of wind.

Heavy footsteps tramped down the tunnel.

I don't feel right, I said, lying down.

I should think not. You shot yourself in the head.

That's not what happened, I said.

The shadows in the cave lengthened, stirred towards me. Like the inky crenulations thrown by ash limbs against the wall of a street lamp-lit room, or the giants in my nightmares wading through sulphurous light, the figures surrounded me and pressed down on me. *Haman was hanged on the very gallows that he had built for Mordecai.* The yellow jackets gleamed through the gloom, I could see them from where I lay, like the golden headlights of Parisian cars in the sixties. The *gilets jaunes* want to be seen; to be visible to the invisible powers. It's not too much to ask. In the presence of absence, as Mahmoud Darwish writes about his people, or an honesty-seeking response, as Gershom Scholem writes about his. All I want is to disappear. In the entry to this frowsty antre. Shadows on M. Platon's wall. What use to me Alice Crary's non-neutral conception of reality; what use to me Dworkin *et aliae* kicking the pricks of patriarchy? What now grips my guts, punts my uterus, scythes me, episiotomy, splits my vagina with its piss-yellow amniotic fluid-anointed head pushing out of my cervix through my own blood and shit into the dirt of life? I chose not to choose this. Not on the floor of this cave, which is the floor of all caves. In adamantine chains and penal fire. With floods and whirlwinds of tempestuousness. My chloasmatic face. The funic souffle in my ears. *Abruptio placentae.* Featly done, doctor! But to what had I not-given birth? In the ruck of animalcules crawling towards me I saw the entrails of a seraphim called Ashtaroth or Astoreth or Astarte or maybe there was wax in my ears again. Something with an A.

Bend low, H!

How comes it, then, that thou art out of hell?
Why, this is hell, nor am I out of it.

Once more I felt a pinpoint of pain in my right arm from a needle or a syringe. Before everything went dark, I heard someone say: The great aurochs is dead.

Never trust a child.

73

I floated in and out of consciousness, like a character in an epic poem by an eighteenth-century tyro who only appears when the rhyme requires her. There was the sense of movement, as Thom Gunn might say. And of light – many colours: purple, burnt orange, lilac, terre verte, sienna, cerulean, golden yellow, violet – and of sound – many sources: rushing water, wild wind, murmuring voices, heavy footsteps, the susurrus of car wheels over a well-built road.

Here is a picture of a subfusc autoroute in France:

At length I woke in a dim room the nature of which at first I could not discern. As my eyes adjusted to the gloom, I saw there were two small windows with metal grilles high up on the walls, a wooden chair painted white, and a broken mirror, roughly trapezoidal in shape. On the door to the room was a peephole about twenty centimetres square that operated on a shutter system with a hinged leaf and five heavy iron slats that pivoted on their horizontal axes. The walls were smooth and white. The windows, which were on the wall opposite the heavy gunmetal-grey door, were so high up and the masonry in which they were cut was so thick, that I could see nothing but the interior of the wall – the top and sides of the horizontal shaft leading, presumably, to open air. Occasionally I thought I heard the cry of a gull, or the dull boom of nearby surf. But this could as easily have been piped in over speakers concealed high up in the walls.

I know there were speakers because occasionally they would crackle to life and I would hear a distorted voice ask me questions or shout commands.

Error in the text! Punishment!

I didn't respond.

Does the word rutilant mean to you the same thing as red?

Sure, I said.

Thank you, it was useful to have that clarified.

Sure, I said.

Why didn't you speak about the traffic noise sooner?

It had nothing to do with the matter in question, I replied, trying to be reasonable.

For hours I would be left alone, lying on my cot, staring at the slats of the peephole. At one point I noticed, in my obsessive recapitulation of the spare ornaments of my room, that the heavy gunmetal-grey door was not flush with the wall; that is to say it was not wholly closed, by a matter of some millimetres. Because I had grown tired of the endless rounds of drugging and interrogation – not to mention the lack of proper nourishment – I decided that the best option was to escape.

I got up and went to the door. Pushing against it with the weight of my body, I found to my surprise that the door swung open smoothly, giving onto a dark corridor. The only light came from back inside my room, but I decided to close the door to prevent for as long as possible the discovery of my absence. I proceeded by hugging the wall several metres to my right. The wall was smooth and the floor free of obstacles, but after approximately ten metres (it's difficult to judge distances in the dark) I ran into the end of the hallway, which turned at a right angle into another, slightly narrower hallway, with rougher walls and rubble-strewn ground. The darkness lessened slightly; I thought I could detect a faint light source round the next corridor, some twenty metres ahead. I made my way towards that corner, which was also set at a right angle, and again narrower; the light grew stronger towards the end, and I decided to head towards it. The ground now became muddier, and there were muddy depressions and large stones in the path.

I noticed on the ground in front of me handprints and footprints in the mud, and a high-heeled shoe, blue-green, heel broken. It looked like a left shoe, and about my size. Shots rang out behind me, at irregular intervals, which caused me to drop the shoe and continue faster, crouched low to the ground but upright, running, picking my way round the mud puddles and rocks until I came to the end of the corridor, which angled again to the right, and dead-ended on a heavy gunmetal-grey door.

I went up to the door, which was locked but which had in place of a doorknob or handle or lock the same strange upside-down eye inside a triangle that I had seen in front of the cave entrance in the Grésivaudan valley. I felt inside the pocket of my silk robe, and, sure enough, there was the thin metallic device I'd used to activate the hand scanner. I pressed the device and the door hinged open. As it did, gun-fire again broke out again behind me, and a woman screamed in pain. I stepped inside the door, which shut behind me.

That's how I found myself back in my apartment. Before I had time to process what had happened, someone pounded on my door. I crossed the room and opened it, and there you were.

No, hold on. That's what it says, but that's not how it happened. When I stepped into my apartment and closed the door behind me, I first went straight to my laptop and wrote Chapter 73. Automatically, without reflection. When I got to the end of the chapter you knocked on my door. I shouldn't have written *pounded* because you weren't pounding. You were knocking. But pounded fit better with the description of my escape, so I wrote pounded.

I put the manuscript down and looked over at Juno.

How about another drink? I asked. I recommend a round of Singani mojitos.

MOJITO

2 OZ SINGANI 63
JUICE OF HALF A LIME
HANDFUL OF FRESH MINT
.75 OZ BROWN SUGAR
3 DASHES ANGOSTURA BITTERS
CLUB SODA

MUDDLE MINT AND BROWN SUGAR.
ADD SINGANI 63 AND LIME JUICE AND
SHAKE WITH ICE. POUR INTO A HIGHBALL
GLASS AND FILL WITH ICE. TOP WITH
CLUB SODA, BITTERS AND MINT.

I handed her the drink, and she smiled as she took it, sipped politely, made a noise of appreciation, then set it down on top of a copy of *Artforum* on my coffee table.

Is that part true, where you said Francesca Woodman jumped out of this apartment? she asked.

Yes, I said. Off the roof. It looked a lot different back in 1981. Her space would have been smaller and the windows smaller too.

Huh. That's—

Can I say, by the way, how winsome your skin looks? I said. It reminds me of Rubens' *Le Chapeau de Paille*.

The one in the National Portrait Gallery? In St Martin's Place?

That's the one! You've seen it then?

It's one of my favourite Rubens, Juno said. But you're too sweet. Just be glad you don't have my hair.

She shook her head, triggering a recoil of golden ringlets around her shoulders. It did look hard to domesticate. But it was probably clean.

It's probably clean, I said. I can't remember the last time I washed my hair. I could remember clearly, it was in the hotel in Grenoble, but I couldn't be sure how long ago that was. It was quicker to say I couldn't remember.

Wasn't it in the hotel room in Grenoble? Juno said. When H1 knocked on your door and didn't get any of your painting references.

I forgot that she'd just listened to me read the manuscript.

She picked up the copy of Robbe-Grillet's *Recollections of the Golden Triangle* in the T. E. Breunn translation and flipped to the end.

What did I say? What did I do?

Qu'ai-je dit? Qu'ai-je fait? I parroted in French.

Sorry, I don't speak French. My mother does, she's practically fluent, but somehow I've never had the time, said Juno.

I was saying the same thing you did, but in French. The last words of Robbe-Grillet's book.

A huge gust of wind threw up a scrabble of litter and pebbles against my window. Something that may have been a bird but was possibly also a woman's shoe – it was a flash of light blue, then it was gone – bounced off the glass with a thud.

Hurricane-proof, I murmured, dully.

A storm is blowing in from paradise, Juno said.

The angel of history. Such a sad image, I find.

We observed a moment of silence thinking about the burning of Notre Dame and the shutting down of CBGB.

Anyway, I think it's marvellous. Just – you know, fucking awesome.

Walter Benjamin? I said.

No, your book. What you read.

I had suddenly lost interest in the book.

Do you ever feel that life is a story you tell yourself over and over until it comes true? I asked.

I always feel that way, Juno said.

Why did you knock on my door in the first place? I asked. It occurred to me to ask. No, I asked. Better the first time.

I thought I heard screaming. After what happened with your friend Thomas—

I'm glad you knocked. And I value your feedback. I've just finished writing, and when you shut yourself up for a long time you can lose your sense of reality. Certainly I can't be objective about its merits.

I know what you mean. When I'm done with a shoot, I have no idea whether the film will be a total disaster or a huge hit. Usually it's neither.

And you never worked with my sister.

Considering she doesn't exist, I can definitely answer 'no'.

I had forgotten that I'd made up Angelica. What else had I invented?

The power of the imagination to transform memory. Not for nothing is Mnemosyne the mother of the muses. In that brief syncope, I wondered if it would ever be possible again to listen to *Kind of Blue* the way people listened to it when it first came out.

. . . Violet, said Juno.

I'm sorry, what? I asked.

I am a poor host.

I was saying, Juno said, my middle name is Violet. Like your name.

My name—

Though I was reasonably certain that John McEnroe was the Wimbledon champion in 1981, beating Björn Borg in four sets, 6–4 in the fourth, I could not recall my own name.

I tried to say as much to Juno, but she had disappeared.

Now we'll never get to make out. I could tell she wanted to. Or at least, I wanted to, and it has almost always been my experience that whatever I want, the other person wants too, provided the other person is what I want.

I say of our melancholy man, he is the cream of human adversity, the quintessence, and upshot; all other diseases whatsoever are but flea-bitings to melancholy in extent; 'tis the pith, nub, core, crux, essence of them all.

Hospitium est calamitalis; quid verbis opus est?
Quamcunque malam rem quaeris, illic reperies:

And a melancholy man is that true Prometheus, which is bound to Caucasus; the true Tityus, whose bowels are still by a vulture devoured, for so doth Lilius Giraldus interpret it, and so ought it to be understood. Some make a question whether the diseases of the body or the mind be more grievous, but there is no comparison or doubt to be made of it, the diseases of the mind are much more grievous.

Wherefore hath our Mother Earth brought out poisons, saith Pliny, in so great a quantity, but that men in distress might make away themselves?

The windows at the front of my apartment shattered as under the force of an immense hammer blow, and I turned to see a vortex of glass and paper whirl in slow motion round my apartment, centred, it seemed to me, on myself. Like Peter Weir's *The Last Wave* but without the water. Are all memories *d'outre-tombe*, M. Chateaubriand? Is all broderie anglaise, Mrs Trefusis? They shoot horses, don't they, Mr McCoy? The shell of myself, imbricated by the books I have read over time, flew apart in the air, joined the whirling glass and paper in an onomastic dance; my gimcrack furniture broke apart, the walls, made of books, disintegrated. The *Legenda aurea* of Jacobus da Varagine says nothing to me about my life, but he was not hanged upside down and burned at the stake, and in Ottaviano Nelli's fresco at Trinci Palaci in Foligno he appears at the side of the crucified Christ holding a copy of his book. I don't know if he managed to sell any copies that day, but it's not *just* about sales.

This only let me add, that in some cases those hard censures of such as offer violence to their own persons, or in some desperate fit to others, which sometimes they do by stabbing, slashing, etc., are to be mitigated, as in such as are mad, beside themselves for the time (as I now find myself), or found to have been long in extreme melancholy.

Swedenborg wrote in *Arcana Cœlestia* that *not only faith, but also the Lord himself is called the seed of the woman, both because He alone gives faith, and because He was pleased to be born.* Thomas Browne in *The Garden of Cyrus* wrote *the quincunx of heaven runs low, and 'tis time to close the five ports of knowledge.* I am not well versed in the spectrum of Swedenborgian thought, and it's been a while since I read *Religio Medici* – and now I'll never have the chance to revisit. But I'm confident in declaring those two commendable men full to their sockets (though in the case of Thomas Browne, whereabouts of skull and thus sockets unknown according to W. G. Sebald at the time of writing *The Rings of Saturn*, and I'm not in a position at present to follow up) of shit. Voices carry, and we've carried enough of yours, guys. We've carried enough voices to last until the end of the world, which insofar as it concerns human beings is closer than we are willing to admit on our darkest nights in our darkest thoughts. World Fever isn't a disease. We're the disease, and World Fever is the cure.

I do miss that Hilma af Klint painting. She painted for the future. She knew then what everyone else is finding out now: the future has already happened. The future passed us by. Didn't even wave.

Fuck the fucking future.

77

Francesca Woodman jumped from a window in my apartment in 1981, twelve years before I was born. She was only twenty-two years old. But I don't want to mislead you: her suicide is not what makes her interesting to me. Her work is what attracts me, what convinced me to buy this particular apartment in this particular building, which is otherwise not in actual fact conveniently sited for my few (fewer all the time) needs. I hoped that by literally inhabiting her former space, I could better understand the importance of her work to me, to my work, to the conceptual framework through which by careful study I have half-deciphered the world.

Woodman took a lot of photographs of herself, often in the nude but not always. In many of her photographs there's some kind of distortion of the fabric of reality – most often by using very long exposures at a time when using very long exposures was unusual for the type of portraiture she undertook. The effect is almost always spectral, blurred, but never exhibitionist or sensational – precisely the opposite. In almost every one of her auto-portraits, Francesca Woodman seems to be trying to figure out how to disappear. The implication is that she's not altogether comfortable with the fact of her existence, but I'm not sure that's right.

Critically adored post-mortem, in roughly the way outlined in Nick Drake's song 'Fruit Tree', Woodman while alive neither sought nor fled what we are legally bound in late-cap Amerika to call *success*. She devoted herself to her work. Her work both sustained and depleted her. This is always the way of it. The only thing special about the manner of her dying was its apparent lack of motivation. This, too, is always the way of it.

I don't as a rule like to say the quiet part loud, but have found via experience that not doing so risks a risk I cannot (dare not?) risk: that one among you might miss the point. If you're wondering why Francesca Woodman chose to take her life on a cold winter day in 1981, I'm more than happy to provide the answer.

78

She jumped for the same reason I jumped, or at least a version of me jumped. These are the facts as I now read them, sadly no longer to Juno Temple.

Some translation of myself, though not the original, the one that the illiterate world considers me, is lying crumpled on the sidewalk outside the building in the East Village of New York City where I have lived for the last few years in a loft apartment on the fifth floor. That copy of myself – let's call her V2, though she prefers Violet, but it's my book – was sitting at her desk working on a spec translation of Robbe-Grillet's *Souvenirs du triangle d'or* when the phone rang. That's the last thing V2 remembers concretely and in detail as her own memory before the devil possessed her. Blood is gathering in thick black puddles around her head.

By jumping off the roof of my building to the street below, V2 hoped to get rid of the devil (not necessarily *the* devil, certainly *a* devil, or demon, or dybbuk) that she believes possessed her. It worked, but the problem is, she's dead.

Let's go now to V2, dead on the scene.

Being dead is pretty boring. I haven't dislodged from the spot where I landed when I jumped off the roof. My limbs are broken in several places and stick out at weird angles. The part of my face that landed on the street is crushed. I can detach myself from my body and manoeuvre – it's hard to know the right word for this, maybe emanate? – to a vertical position about three metres in any direction from my body but I am tied to my body somehow. I don't feel particularly floaty or light, in other words my emanation, if that's what we're calling it, has substance but is also clearly not substantial, and is not visible to other people. A crowd is clustered around my body. People are filming or taking pictures of my corpse with their phones. In the distance I can hear sirens, but whether those sirens are for me or just quotidian New York City sirens is impossible to predict.

Which brings me to another topic. Nothing is happening. These people, these cars, these sounds, this air: it's frozen, but frozen isn't the right word, because there's some flexibility, some movement, and I can hear the sirens, which doesn't make sense if the sirens are part of time, which they would have to be.

Oh, also, I can move *through* time. I can move through the past. I can't go forward, I can't go into the future, anyway I haven't figured out how. Moving through the past is easy. You swipe your hands like the world was a screen and scroll through, as slowly or as quickly as you want. I can't peregrinate through space, so I'm limited to the past as it relates to the few metres of my circumscribed being, but when has that not been true? But I can go back. I can go to the past.

I can go back to the beginning. The beginning of everything. I've seen it: the so-called Big Bang. It's not what I expected. I went back before that. Before time. You can do that. Before time was, before space was: I've been there. I'm there right now. There and not there, if that makes sense.

In conclusion: *Pedicabo ego vos et irrumabo*. Wretched, wicked Catullus. *Omnia vincit amor*. Stupid, vicious Virgil.

In conclusion: everything has its shadow.

In conclusion: *Pour vivre heureux, vivons cachés*, wrote Jean-Pierre Claris de Florian in his fable/poem 'Le Grillon', freely adapting Ovid's *Bene qui latuit, bene vixit* (*Tristia*), and you would do well to mind or mine those words, as Descartes earlier did, although he got the word order wrong. *Je suis donc je pense*. Not those words. Those words are a joke.

In conclusion: you are connected to the immaterial material of the universe by invisible but unbreakable bonds.

In conclusion: remember the swans. The swans are important.

Here is an illustration of the meaning of life:

You will have noticed a dot in the centre of the spiral on the previous page. That dot has been impregnated, if impregnated is the word I want, with a highly concentrated dose of the most potent hallucinogenic drug on earth: LSD-75x. If you will but cut the dot out of the spiral and place it on or under your tongue, within one to two hours – depending on your body size, weight, age and your familiarity with and/or fondness for the poetry of Louise Bogan – you will find the meaning of life legible. Please remember to pay particular attention to what the experts call set and setting, which is to say that you should be somewhere you feel comfortable, and you should yourself be physically comfortable. Having a friend to watch over you while you understand the meaning of life can be helpful, as this understanding can easily cause you to go insane, and insane people sometimes behave in ways deleterious to long life and good health. If you can't have a friend watch over you – maybe, like me, you don't have any friends – then I'd advise strapping yourself down or otherwise restricting your movements so that in the event that you do go insane you will not harm yourself or others.

Also recommended: before taking the dose of LSD-75x, you should get a tattoo of the spiral on the previous page on your left shoulder or right ankle. It's not essential, but it will help. If you happen to be reading this on a screen instead of on the page, and want to understand the meaning of life, it will be necessary to send a stamped, self-addressed envelope to the publisher of this book, who will supply you with your black dot. I have arranged for a nearly illimitable supply, so you should not feel impelled to rush to send in your envelope out of fear that we will run out of black dots. But we will need the stamped, self-addressed envelope because, while everyone's happy to supply the world twice over with black dots, you'll agree that it's unreasonable to expect us to bear the full expense of the operation. If the publisher of this book for some reason no longer exists, if, for instance, you are reading this a hundred years in the future and book publishers no longer exist, or books, or recognisably human civilisation, and you still wish to understand the meaning of life, I have made contingencies, because if we've learned one thing from J.-P. Sartre it's that we are free, and something about contingencies.

Whether you are able to access the LSD-75x or not, you should try repeating the Latin phrase you read at the beginning of the book: *Est aliquid prodisse tenus.* This can be translated as *It is something to have come out.* Or more colloquially as: *Hey, we made a start.* The phrase occurs in the *De monade numero et figura* of Giordano Bruno, the sixteenth-century Hermetic occultist who was hung upside down and burned at the stake, and by reading it you have been possessed by the demon, or devil, that I exorcised by jumping off the roof of my building.

81

Sorry. Sorry about that. There was no other way. That's why I went back in time and put the words at the beginning of the book, to ensure that there was no way for you to avoid seeing them. You don't have to say them out loud or read them to be possessed; you have to see them. And now you have.

A few words about that.

Things are going to start to happen. Whether you like it or not, you have been inducted into the Order of the Golden Triangle. I've given you a fairly detailed outline of what lies in store, but ymmv. I advise cutting the dot out of the spiral and ingesting the LSD-75x asap. It will help lessen the shock of the things that are going to start to happen. But it won't prevent them from happening. No way around that, I'm afraid. The part you will find hardest to deal with, I suspect, is that you won't notice that things are happening. Your life will proceed in its usual fashion. To you, to anyone else, you will not look or act possessed in any of the ways Hollywood or the Bible or books in general or the internet or possibly your own imagination have led you to believe. You will be and feel yourself. You will nevertheless be possessed by the devil, or a devil, there's a little confusion on this point. She calls herself Belzébeth, also sometimes Griselda, Brunelda and Lady Caroline. Once also Virginie, and there was a reference to a Nathalie, but I may have misheard. That's all I know. I'm sure the extremely online among you can dig up more demon-related intel, and I wish you well in your endeavours. Maybe she's on Twitter. It's more than likely she's on Twitter.

The Order of the Golden Triangle, I will not lie, is among other things a sex cult, so you should be prepared for some heavy S&M action that for all I know you might enjoy. You will also be required to turn over your dreams to their research unit. I'm told they're doing interesting work in that area, related to AI, which in turn plays a big role in the sex cult. As with any efficiently run organisation, everything feeds into everything else, and there's the purely fiscal aspect, which is not inconsiderable. If you come across a guy named Dr Morgan, run as fast as you can in the opposite direction.

'The Wreck of the Hesperus' spirals to mind, as does the Bermuda Triangle, *L'Écume des jours*, Ibn al-Arabi, Clarice Lispector, hypostasis, the use of magnetoreception by salmon when returning to spawn, H. Rider Haggard, Eric Dolphy, a grey pelican, hauntology, Eve Babitz, the misuses of enchantment, Jessamyn West, the phoenix on the ceiling of my hotel in Cap Ferret, Anthony Braxton, Daša Drndić, Antinous, the Peculiar People, Sophie Calle, the paintings of Brueghel the Elder, troll farms and, as always, poor Francesca Woodman. I've met her. You can't interact with people from the past – I mean you can, but it freaks them out, they think you're a ghost – but in this case I have made an exception.

By now I have developed the ability to extend as far as one hundred metres in physical space, as well as travel through time. I revealed myself to Francesca Woodman (which is to say myself), and I told her what I told you when we began.

A metaphor is a ladder to the truth but is not itself true.

Then I pulled away the ladder, and she fell.

```
FIN FIN FIN                              FIN FIN FIN
FIN FIN FIN                             FIN FIN FIN
FIN FIN FIN                            FIN FIN FIN
 FIN FIN FIN                          FIN FIN FIN
  FIN FIN FIN                        FIN FIN FIN
   FIN FIN FIN                      FIN FIN FIN
    FIN FIN FIN                    FIN FIN FIN
     FIN FIN FIN                  FIN FIN FIN
      FIN FIN FIN                FIN FIN FIN
       FIN FIN FIN              FIN FIN FIN
        FIN FIN FIN            FIN FIN FIN
         FIN FIN FIN          FIN FIN FIN
          FIN FIN FIN        FIN FIN FIN
           FIN FIN FIN      FIN FIN FIN
            FIN FIN FIN    FIN FIN FIN
             FIN FIN FIN  FIN FIN FIN
              FIN FIN FIN FIN FIN FIN
              FIN FIN FIN FIN FIN FIN
               FIN FIN FIN FIN FIN
               FIN FIN FIN FIN FIN
                FIN FIN FIN FIN
                FIN FIN FIN FIN
```

HELP DESK

What is the nouveau roman? Literally, 'new novel', a loosely organised movement of French novelists working in the fifties and sixties who rejected many of the accepted features of the novel. The phrase was coined by a clearly bored French journalist in the newspaper *Le Monde* in 1957. Arguably its leading practitioner, or at least theorist, Alain Robbe-Grillet (see entry on R-G) put forward a theory of the novel as focused on objects: the ideal *nouveau roman*, in his view, would subordinate plot and character to a microscopic, some might even say tedious, examination of the details of the novelist's constructed word-world.

Who is Not Michel Houellebecq? Not the author of several novels disparate in subject matter but often guided by an enthusiasm for provocation. He has never been accused at various times over his long career (by doubtless morally pristine critics) as a vulgar, racist, obscene, Islamophobic misogynist. He does not share with Alain Robbe-Grillet a fascination with the sex life of the adult heteronormative male human. He is not extremely unattractive.

What is the 'impulse towards irony'? The idea of 'the impulse towards irony' as the defining characteristic of human beings occurred to me when I was reading Dostoevsky, specifically

(I think, I don't have access to my books at present, being more or less dead) *Notes from Underground*, as the title is often inaccurately translated in English. He spoke, or his main character did, same thing, of the ability of a person to say that 2+2=5, even though he or she or it knew full well that 2+2=4, simply out of a contrarian or spiteful impulse – in other words to act knowingly and wilfully against one's own interest – as the primary distinction of the human being. Another example from the same book (paraphrased): I am free to bash my head into a brick wall, knowing that it will hurt like hell, knowing that I may in fact be putting my life at risk, for precisely that reason: because I can. And no other creature on earth has that ability. To act irrationally, on purpose. To embrace the irrational. These are extreme examples but illustrative.

Where did the title Bad Eminence *come from?* From *Paradise Lost.* That's all the clueing-in you get.

Who was Alain Robbe-Grillet? French director, novelist, critic, bondage enthusiast, pervert (1922–2008). His book *Souvenirs du triangle d'or* – not one of his better-known novels – is the raw material for much of what passes for the plot of *Bad Eminence.* He was a little too fond of young girls even at a time when over-fondness for young girls was practically an entrance requirement for French letters.

What are troll farms? Usually located in the desert wastes of Utah, these are factory-type farms where trolls are grown. Trolls can reach the size of mature eggplants, but rarely live long enough to exceed the size of a lima bean.

Who was Ross Macdonald? A California-centric crime writer, best known for his Lew Archer series, from whom I have stolen some of the best words used in this book. I ask you, then, who's the real crime writer here?

Who was Fiat Lux? Author most notably of the novel *Artificial Light*. One of our greatest living writers. Except that she may not be living. It's unclear. She disappeared in 2006 or so.

What is the Malleus Maleficarum? Usually Englished as *The Witches' Hammer*, it's a really cool video game invented in the fifteenth century by Thorgild Ragamuffin. The object of the game is to hit witches on the head with a hammer until they are all dead. Alternatively, you can set them on fire, hang them by the neck and then set them on fire, or drown them in the nearest body of water (after they've been dredged up and dried off, you can still set them on fire). Includes a handy 'How to Identify a Witch' guide, which in essence tells you that any woman who annoys you, however slightly, for whatever reason, is clearly a witch. Checks out.

Who is Eve Babitz? Juniper, oak and sweet gum. A frosted window, the arc of a barn swallow against the pale sky at dusk. I could go on.

Who is Juno Temple? British-born actress, daughter of the director Julien Temple; my upstairs neighbour; very good at rarely returning my emails or texts and at inexplicably disappearing from my NYC loft in mid-sentence. Current whereabouts unknown.

What is I Am Your Sister? A book of posthumous, previously uncollected and/or unpublished writings by Audre Lorde, a brilliant poet and thinker.

Who are Death Hags? Possibly the greatest musical artist on the face of the earth, now and forever, but you wouldn't know that because you have no (or possibly just underdeveloped) taste in music.

What is Céline et Julie vont en bateau? A film by Jacques Rivette that you should stop everything and watch right now.

What is L'Écume des jours? An extended unfunny joke by the French writer Boris Vian. No, that's not fair. It's not actually extended. It's exactly the right length. And some people do find it funny, or at least interesting. Required reading for French *lycée* students of a certain era, which may explain my antipathy. I don't like being told what to read.

Who was Francesca Woodman (1958–1981)? American photographer. Born in Denver, educated at the Rhode Island School of Design, moved to NYC in 1979. Prior to her suicide, she had published very little of her work, but in the ensuing years she has experienced a well-justified surge of interest in her mysterious and boundary-pushing work. Her photograph unofficially titled *Leda and the Swan* is the wing beneath the wind of this book.

Who was Hilma af Klint? A pawnshop ghost inside a garbage can.

What is the secret of life? Darkness inside the muted light of sunset: when you stand in front of the window and stare at the far hills. These are the bad angels, gathering in gloomy bunches like poisonous grapes, deep purple with blood. The leafless trees scratch with upstretched arms at scudding clouds, and in the growing mist barn owls perch on lower branches, scanning the radio air for the slow heartbeat of approaching doom. The bad angels grasp in their grasping claws the agenda of nightmares, larded with entrails of dead shrubs and bits of Styrofoam and brick. You roll the heavy door across its track and fasten tight the locks. You know that nothing made of something can stop the angels, who are nothing. You've looked them in the eye and seen the end of time, and the end of time was a mirror. And still you roll the door, and still you light the fat candle, and the wax drips forest green on the polished marble floor: you turn and find yourself inside a tomb, which is where you keep the rain, for safety.

But you are not safe. The rain cannot keep you bright for long, and your tears will only fall, unseen. There are corridors in this place that lead to holy places, but all the holy places have been destroyed, out of love, out of a desire to love that burns without burning – a plague of love, a cholera of kindness. Dig a ditch and wait for pistol shot in back of neck. Or is that too romantic? Would you prefer a meaner death? Shrivelling for years in the data basement, in an old hard drive, dispersing bit by bit on the ocean floor of knowledge, frozen, unexplored, blind, pressed flat by calamitous gravity.

The *Periplus* and Rhapta. Arab and Indian traders looking for gold in the first of twenty long centuries. Is this what you mean by Africa? The devil is no fool. Why fear the means of grace, expel yourself from your own garden? Difficult to till, ravaged by bad angels, daily exposed to the secrets of flight. You think because everything has roots that nothing can fly? The last thing out of the chest, children, was a very fragile creature, its tiny hairs still slick with afterbirth. You must do your best to keep it alive.

Who was Mr Powell's Delavaquerie? A character from Anthony Powell's magisterial [one is required by state law in the state I'm currently in, which I am not allowed to disclose, as a further requirement of state law in the state I'm in, to use the word 'magisterial' whenever referencing Powell's work] *A Dance to the Music of Time*, a series of twelve sequential novels, which was very popular back in the 1940s, '50s and '60s, I'm told, by people who were alive in the '40s, '50s and '60s. Highly recommended if you need to kill a year.

What is OULIPO? Short for *Ouvroir de littérature potentielle*, which you can approximate in English as Workshop of Potential Literature (it makes as little sense in French). A French movement that, as its name suggests, attempted to construct new forms of literature by imposing arbitrary constraints within which the writer was free to do whatever he or she or they wanted to do. Its two best known exemplars are probably the aforementioned (in the text) Georges Perec's *La disparition*, a novl writtn without th us of th lttr ' ', and Raymond Queneau's *Exercices de style*, wherein he retells the same very short, very banal story ninety-nine times, using a different style for each retelling. Sort of a potted version of the many stylistic parodies employed by Joyce in *Ulysses*, without all the hard work. Writers love this kind of shit. Readers, not so much. For Queneau, read *Zazie dans le Métro* instead. A much better book.

What is a roman de gare? Literally, a 'train-station novel', so-called because they are commonly sold at train stations in France. Usually a pulp novel or detective fiction of putatively little literary merit, much like 'airport novels' in the US. Past the mossy ruin of the old watermill, evidence of human resistance, evidence of futility, of abandonment. The river changed course over not much time. Remained only a shallow stream several metres away, near-buried in upgrowth of bunchberry and wood sorrel. You can hear more than see it, though there were gaps that glinted darkly in the early light. Hints of water, really. Astuces. What you do with these answers is your own business.

Who was Xavier Hadley? Not a real person. Sorry to disappoint.

What is the significance of the swans? We were too young to remember, Thomas Early told us, but in the days before World Fever there was magic in the air. You could turn on a machine and unspool screen after screen of internet, which arrived in your house through microwaves. Everyone had screens not just in their houses but in their pockets, in their hands, screens upon screens unspooling at a word or touch. Sometimes these screens made sounds, sometimes pictures, sometimes both at once, as in the films projected at the warehouse every Oneday. Mostly the screens just told words, like in books, but more than any book, and less susceptible to fire or water. All the words were held in a cloud, bigger than all the clouds in the domed sky on a thunder evening, bigger than the land, bigger than the sea, or very nearly. Big as air, were these clouds.

What is the point of Los Angeles? We try to pretend nothing has happened, and what, after all, has happened? The ruby-throat still darts between the orange and violet bird-of-paradise, the rosemary still flowers pale in the spring, and soon, though not soon enough, the jacaranda trees will bloom. We are a regal city, from our grandiose name to the profusion of royal purple in which we drape ourselves from the low hills at the coast to the flatlands of the Inland Empire.

What is Le Jardin des supplices? The word 'ant' is derived from Old English by way of Proto-German, and originally meant 'the biter'. It's a good Anglo-Saxon word, and one of those rare words that exactly fits its subject. Cow is another good word. You might think a three-letter word too small to contain such a beast (beast is another good one), but the stretched 'o' supported on the one side by a sturdy consonant and the other by the down-filled pillows of its 'w' suit the lowing or bellowing or just plain mooing cow to a 't'. Making a moot point of the notion that a cow is stupid. Nothing beautiful is stupid, not even the moon-faced sunflower, despite attempts by certain writers who shall not be named and shamed here to state otherwise. Everybody makes mistakes. Even Octave Mirbeau.

Who is Michael Stipe? Purportedly the singer in a no-longer-extant pop group called R.E.M., trendy among college students in the 1980s. Gifted with a preternaturally deep speaking voice. Can be funny when he wants, but never as funny as he thinks he is. Which is true of most people, come to think of it.

What's Behind the Green Door? Oscar Delacroix, no relation (sitting in Les Grandes Marches under L'Opéra Bastille with a good view of the bustling *place* and its central figure – Liberty, or something), is barely present. She stops writing, puts down her pen. Takes one lump of *sucre roux* from the saucer and drops it into her espresso. Picks up a spoon and stirs, gently. She never looks to see if the lump (*le morceau*) hits or misses the cup, which is after all not large, nor does she bother to determine with her spoon whether the lump (*le morceau*) has dissolved completely before raising the cup to her lips and taking a sip.

Oscar has been making a list in her notebook of the things that break her heart: 1) Girl in pleated, dark-blue skirt who removes her glasses with left hand, carelessly, slips one arm in her shirt pocket, turns from a bookstore window to greet a friend. She was looking at Pinget's *Mahu*, which (typically) did not look back. Books are too proud. No wonder no one reads. 2) The undertow of melancholy that tugs at her stomach when the light is low and slanted through Porte Saint-Denis and couples drink on gaslit *terrasses.* 3) How dust motes and dust mites denote two very different things: the former unspeakably lovely, the latter ugly and pathogenic.

What is Singani 63? Singani is a Bolivian *eau-de-vie* or brandy distilled from white Muscat of Alexandria grapes. Only produced in the high valleys of Bolivia, it is the country's national distilled spirit and considered part of its cultural patrimony. Singani 63 is the imported-to-the-US version of that liquor. It's extremely smooth, contains no additives or sulfites or really anything bad whatsoever, can be mixed with literally anything but also tastes great straight from the gd bottle. It should really be classified as medicine, because it's good for what ails ya.

What is Intercourse? If you mean the book by Andrea Dworkin, then it's a book by Andrea Dworkin. If you mean fucking, then it's fucking.

Who was Susan Sontag? You have to be kidding. You don't know who Susan Sontag was? Jesus. I give up.

What is The Waves? When Routledge Ruut stood, alone and smoking in the middle of the desolate battlefield, he could not see the parts of bodies or the writhing and groaning recently human forms, he could not see or hear anything in fact, blind from the blood caked over his eyes and deaf from the cannon's shout, but he could see in his mind the yellow rose he had grown in a small clay pot on his windowsill earlier that year.

That rose was long bloomed, and the clay pot shattered or consumed by fire when the enemy troops ravaged the town. And yet. If a thing can be held in the mind and regarded with precision, passionately held by force of will as if the eye were present, then no separate reality existed which could overthrow the one so constructed.

Who is Patti Smith? A well-known horse breeder, whose photos of (occasionally golden) palominos have achieved worldwide renown after one of them was chosen for the cover of *Horse Fancier* magazine, now defunct. Not to be confused with the punk rock icon and quondam poet and memoirist. Although, weirdly, they both dated Sam Shepard.

Who is Bartleby? With respect to film and music, almost all forms of dissemination of recorded product heretofore have involved circular objects, spinning. No matter how far back you look. Revolvers, each and every one, but no more. I don't these days know the shape of the medium. Does anyone? Is there a shape? I have seen certain media represented as a waveform, but I suspect that waveform is merely a visual translation of a shapeless batch of numbers.

'Bartleby the Scrivener' is the name of a short story written by Herman Melville, whose titular character has been given the catchphrase 'I would prefer not to'. Melville was way ahead of his time in assigning catchphrases to characters.

What is 'Elegy Written in a Country Churchyard'? A poem by Thomas Gray. It does not go like this, but it does go *with* this:

> Sycamore, sycamore, rock. The trees
> Lean against me; winter's fluff
> Sits owlish on their crowns. Moon sees
> Beak of shivered alpine chough

As bait. Outside each house a clock
Runs independently of time—
Splits the hours from a stock
Of solid sorrow, hung from lime
Branch like despondent gems, grief-
Bright with pending tears. Why wait
To say goodbye, why not unleaf
The rake of going soon than late,
Or better still scrape from debris
Homunculus of me. No words
Will ever pass its lips. The birds
Above are swallows: irony.

How do you stop an elevator from stopping? Don't let's start.

Can you explain Out to Lunch!, *Eric Dolphy's jazz masterpiece?*
The banquet was in honour of my life but was also a ravening
of my life. The meat and drink were my words and deeds, and
I examined carefully the look on the faces of the guests, to see
whether they were enjoying their meal. Honestly, I couldn't
say. There was not a lot of conversation. The hall was poorly
lit, with a few widely spaced torches throwing weird shadows
across the long oak table, and into the crevices of the stone
walls. An elaborate brass chandelier hung ponderously over
the centre of the table, but none of its candles had been
lighted.

Who was Nancy Wake (the White Mouse)? A New Zealand
woman who somehow ended up in France and joined the
French resistance in WWII, working also with the British

special forces. She was nicknamed 'the White Mouse' by the Nazis for her ability to elude capture. The forest of Tronçais was in the Massif Central near where my grandfather (who reportedly had an affair with her, but that's probably him just post-war bragging) also worked with the Maquis.

Who was Assia Djebar? Pen name of Fatima-Zohra Imalayen (1936–2015), Algerian novelist, translator and film-maker. She was good friends with my mother after her marriage to Malek Alloula and move to Paris in the eighties, though Djebar (or Aunt Fatima, as we were encouraged but usually too scared to call her) was considerably older than my mother. Her anti-colonial and anti-patriarchal attitudes had a pretty big influence on me growing up, though now that I'm quote mature unquote I'm more or less just anti-everything.

Where can I go if I need more help? Straight to hell, pal.

Dear readers,

As well as relying on bookshop sales, And Other Stories relies on sub-scriptions from people like you for many of our books, whose stories other publishers often consider too risky to take on.

Our subscribers don't just make the books physically happen. They also help us approach booksellers, because we can demonstrate that our books already have readers and fans. And they give us the security to publish in line with our values, which are collaborative, imaginative and 'shamelessly literary'.

All of our subscribers:

- receive a first-edition copy of each of the books they subscribe to
- are thanked by name at the end of our subscriber-supported books
- receive little extras from us by way of thank you, for example: postcards created by our authors

BECOME A SUBSCRIBER, OR GIVE A SUBSCRIPTION TO A FRIEND

Visit andotherstories.org/subscriptions to help make our books happen. You can subscribe to books we're in the process of making. To purchase books we have already published, we urge you to support your local or favourite bookshop and order directly from them – the often unsung heroes of publishing.

OTHER WAYS TO GET INVOLVED

If you'd like to know about upcoming events and reading groups (our foreign-language reading groups help us choose books to publish, for example) you can:

- join our mailing list at: andotherstories.org
- follow us on Twitter: @andothertweets
- join us on Facebook: facebook.com/AndOtherStoriesBooks
- admire our books on Instagram: @andotherpics
- follow our blog: andotherstories.org/ampersand

THIS BOOK WAS MADE POSSIBLE
THANKS TO THE SUPPORT OF

Aaron McEnery
Aaron Schneider
Abigail Walton
Adam Lenson
Adrian Kowalsky
Aifric Campbell
Ajay Sharma
Alan McMonagle
Alan Raine
Alastair Gillespie
Alastair Whitson
Albert Puente
Alec Logan
Alex Fleming
Alex Liebman
Alex Lockwood
Alex Pearce
Alex Ramsey
Alex von Feldmann
Alexander Williams
Alexandra Stewart
Alexandra Tammaro
Alexandra Tilden
Alexandra Webb
Ali Ersahin
Ali Smith
Ali Usman
Alice Morgan
Alice Radosh
Alice Smith
Alice Wilkinson
Alison Winston
Alistair Chalmers
Aliya Rashid
Alyssa Rinaldi

Amado Floresca
Amaia Gabantxo
Amanda
Amanda Dalton
Amanda Fisher
Amanda Read
Amine Hamadache
Amitav Hajra
Amy and Jamie
Amy Benson
Amy Bojang
Amy Hatch
Amy Tabb
Ana Novak
Andra Dusu
Andrea Barlien
Andrea Brownstone
Andrea Oyarzabal
   Koppes
Andrew Marston
Andrew McCallum
Andrew Place
Andrew Ratomski
Andrew Reece
Andrew Rego
Andrew Wright
Andy Corsham
Angela Joyce
Angelica Ribichini
Angus Walker
Anita Starosta
Ann Rees
Anna Finneran
Anna French
Anna Gibson

Anna Hawthorne
Anna Milsom
Anna Zaranko
Anne Boileau Clarke
Anne Carus
Anne Craven
Anne Edyvean
Anne Frost
Anne-Marie Renshaw
Anne Ryden
Anne Withane
Annette Hamilton
Annie McDermott
Anonymous
Anonymous
Antonia Lloyd-Jones
Antonia Saske
Antony Osgood
Antony Pearce
Aoife Boyd
April Hernandez
Arabella Bosworth
Arathi Devandran
Archie Davies
Aron Negyesi
Aron Trauring
Arthur John Rowles
Asako Serizawa
Ashleigh Phillips
Audrey Mash
Audrey Small
Barbara Mellor
Barbara Robinson
Barbara Spicer
Barry Norton

Becky Cherriman
Becky Matthewson
Ben Buchwald
Ben Schofield
Ben Thornton
Ben Walter
Benjamin Judge
Benjamin Pester
Bernadette Smith
Beth Heim de Bera
Bianca Duec
Bianca Jackson
Bianca Winter
Bill Fletcher
Bjørnar Djupevik
  Hagen
Blazej Jedras
Brenda Anderson
Briallen Hopper
Brian Anderson
Brian Byrne
Brian Callaghan
Brian Conn
Brian Smith
Brianna Soloski
Bridget Maddison
Bridget Prentice
Buck Johnston
Burkhard Fehsenfeld
Caitlin Halpern
Callie Steven
Cameron Adams
Cameron Lindo
Camilla Imperiali
Carla Castanos
Carole Parkhouse
Carolina Pineiro
Caroline Perry

Caroline Smith
Caroline West
Catharine Braithwaite
Catherine Campbell
Catherine Cleary
Catherine Lambert
Catherine
  Lautenbacher
Catherine Tandy
Catherine Tolo
Catherine Williamson
Cathryn Siegal-
  Bergman
Cathy Galvin
Cathy Sowell
Catie Kosinski
Catrine Bollerslev
Cecilia Rossi
Cecilia Uribe
Chantal Lyons
Chantal Wright
Charlene Huggins
Charles Dee Mitchell
Charles Fernyhough
Charles Kovach
Charles Rowe
Charlie Errock
Charlie Levin
Charlie Small
Charlie Webb
Charlotte Coulthard
Charlotte Furness
Charlotte Holtam
Charlotte Ryland
Charlotte Whittle
Charlotte Woodford
Chenxin Jiang
Cherilyn Elston

China Miéville
Chris Johnstone
Chris Potts
Chris Senior
Chris Stergalas
Chris Stevenson
Chris Thornton
Christian Schuhmann
Christine Bartels
Christopher Allen
Christopher Smith
Christopher Stout
Ciarán Schütte
Claire Adams
Claire Brooksby
Claire Mackintosh
Clarice Borges
Claudia Mazzoncini
Cliona Quigley
Colin Denyer
Colin Hewlett
Colin Matthews
Collin Brooke
Cornelia Svedman
Courtney Lilly
Craig Kennedy
Cris Cucerzan
Cynthia De La Torre
Cyrus Massoudi
Daisy Savage
Dale Wisely
Dan Parkinson
Dana Lapidot
Daniel Gillespie
Daniel Hahn
Daniel Hester-Smith
Daniel Sanford
Daniel Stewart

Daniel Syrovy
Daniel Venn
Daniela Steierberg
Darcie Vigliano
Darryll Rogers
Dave Lander
David Anderson
David Cowan
David Darvasi
David Gould
David Greenlaw
David Gunnarsson
David Hebblethwaite
David Higgins
David Johnson-Davies
David Leverington
David F Long
David Richardson
David Shriver
David Smith
Dawn Bass
Dean Taucher
Deb Unferth
Debbie Enever
Debbie Pinfold
Deborah Green
Deborah Herron
Deborah Wood
Declan Gardner
Declan O'Driscoll
Denis Larose
Derek Sims
Derek Taylor-
    Vrsalovich
Diarmuid Hickey
Dietrich Menzel
Dina Abdul-Wahab
Dinesh Prasad

Domenica Devine
Dominic Bailey
Dominic Nolan
Dominick Santa
    Cattarina
Dominique Hudson
Dornith Doherty
Dorothy Bottrell
Dugald Mackie
Duncan Clubb
Duncan Macgregor
Duncan Marks
Dustin Hackfeld
Dyanne Prinsen
Earl James
Ebba Tornérhielm
Ed Smith
Ed Tronick
Ekaterina Beliakova
Elaine Juzl
Elaine Rodrigues
Eleanor Maier
Elena Esparza
Elif Aganoglu
Elina Zicmane
Eliza Mood
Elizabeth Braswell
Elizabeth Coombes
Elizabeth Draper
Elizabeth Franz
Elizabeth Guss
Elizabeth Leach
Elizabeth Seals
Elizabeth Sieminski
Elizabeth Wood
Ellie Goddard
Emily Paine
Emily Williams

Emma Bielecki
Emma Louise Grove
Emma Post
Emma Teale
Erica Mason
Erin Cameron Allen
Esmée de Heer
Esther Kinsky
Ethan Madarieta
Ethan White
Evelyn Eldridge
Ewan Tant
Fawzia Kane
Fay Barrett
Faye Williams
Felicia Williams
Felix Valdivieso
Finbarr Farragher
Fiona Mozley
Fiona Quinn
Fran Sanderson
Frances Dinger
Frances Harvey
Frances Thiessen
Francesca Brooks
Francis Mathias
Frank Curtis
Frank Rodrigues
Frank van Orsouw
Freddie Radford
Friederike Knabe
Gail Marten
Gala Copley
Gavin Collins
Gawain Espley
Genaro Palomo Jr
Geoff Thrower
Geoffrey Cohen

Geoffrey Urland
George McCaig
George Stanbury
George Wilkinson
Georgia Panteli
Georgia Shomidie
Georgina Norton
Gerry Craddock
Gill Boag-Munroe
Gillian Grant
Gillian Stern
Gina Heathcote
Glenn Russell
Gordon Cameron
Gosia Pennar
Grace Cohen
Graham Blenkinsop
Graham R Foster
Gregor von dem
Knesebeck
Hadil Balzan
Hamish Russell
Hannah Freeman
Hannah Harford-
Wright
Hannah Jane
Lownsbrough
Hannah Rapley
Hanora Bagnell
Hans Lazda
Harriet Stiles
Haydon Spenceley
Hayley Cox
Hazel Smoczynska
Heidi James
Helen Bailey
Helen Berry
Helena Buffery

Henriette Magerstaedt
Henrike Laehnemann
Holly Down
Howard Robinson
Hugh Shipley
Hyoung-Won Park
Ian McMillan
Ian Mond
Ian Randall
Ida Grochowska
Ines Alfano
Irene Croal
Irene Mansfield
Irina Tzanova
Isabella Garment
Isabella Weibrecht
Isobel Foxford
Ivy Lin
JE Crispin
Jacinta Perez Gavilan
Torres
Jack Brown
Jacqueline Haskell
Jacqueline Lademann
Jacqueline Vint
Jacqui Jackson
Jake Baldwinson
Jake Newby
James Attlee
James Avery
James Beck
James Crossley
James Cubbon
James Elkins
James Greer
James Kinsley
James Leonard
James Lesniak

James Portlock
James Ruland
James Scudamore
James Silvestro
Jan Hicks
Jane Anderton
Jane Dolman
Jane Leuchter
Jane Roberts
Jane Roberts
Jane Willborn
Jane Woollard
Janelle Ward
Janis Carpenter
Janna Eastwood
Jasmine Gideon
Jason Montano
Jason Timermanis
Jason Whalley
Jean Liebenberg
Jeanne Guyon
Jeff Collins
Jen Hardwicke
Jenifer Logie
Jennie Goloboy
Jennifer Fosket
Jennifer Higgins
Jennifer Mills
Jennifer Watts
Jenny Huth
Jenny Newton
Jeremy Koenig
Jerome Mersky
Jess Hazlewood
Jess Howard-Armitage
Jess Wilder
Jess Wood
Jesse Coleman

Jesse Hara
Jessica Gately
Jessica Kibler
Jessica Mello
Jessica Queree
Jethro Soutar
Jill Harrison
Jo Heinrich
Jo Keyes
Jo Pinder
Joanna Luloff
Joao Pedro Bragatti
  Winckler
JoDee Brandon
Jodie Adams
Joe Huggins
Joel Garza
Joel Swerdlow
Joelle Young
Johannes Holmqvist
Johannes Menzel
Johannes Georg Zipp
John Bennett
John Betteridge
John Bogg
John Carnahan
John Conway
John Down
John Gent
John Hodgson
John Kelly
John McWhirter
John Reid
John Shadduck
John Shaw
John Steigerwald
John Wallace
John Walsh

John Winkelman
John Wyatt
Jolene Smith
Jonas House
Jonathan Blaney
Jonathan Fiedler
Jonathan Harris
Jonathan Huston
Jonathan Phillips
Joni Chan
Jonny Kiehlmann
Jordana Carlin
Jorid Martinsen
Joseph Schreiber
Joseph Thomas
Josh Sumner
Joshua Davis
Judith Gruet-Kaye
Judith Hannan
Judith Virginia Moffatt
Judith Poxon
Judy Davies
Judy Rich
Julia Rochester
Julia Von Dem
  Knesebeck
Julian Hemming
Julienne van Loon
Juliet Birkbeck
Jupiter Jones
Juraj Janik
Justin Anderson
Justine Goodchild
Justine Sherwood
KL Ee
Kaarina Hollo
Kaelyn Davis
Kaja R Anker-Rasch

Karen Gilbert
Karin Mckercher
Karl Chwe
Katarzyna
  Bartoszynska
Kate Beswick
Kate Carlton-Reditt
Kate Morgan
Kate Procter
Kate Shires
Katharina Liehr
Katharine Robbins
Katherine Brabon
Katherine Sotejeff-
  Wilson
Kathryn Burruss
Kathryn Edwards
Kathryn Williams
Kathy Wright
Katia Wengraf
Katie Brown
Katie Freeman
Katie Grant
Katie Smart
Katy Robinson
Keith Walker
Ken Geniza
Kenneth Blythe
Kent Curry
Kent McKernan
Kerry Parke
Kevin Tole
Kieran Rollin
Kieron James
Kim McGowan
Kirsty Simpkins
Kris Ann Trimis
Kristen Tcherneshoff

Kristin Djuve
Krystale Tremblay-Moll
Krystine Phelps
Kylie Cook
Kyra Wilder
Lacy Wolfe
Lana Selby
Lara Vergnaud
Larry Wikoff
Laura Ling
Laura Newman
Laura Pugh
Laura Zlatos
Lauren Pout
Lauren Rea
Laurence Laluyaux
Lee Harbour
Leona Iosifidou
Leonora Randall
Liliana Lobato
Lily Blacksell
Linda Milam
Lindsay Brammer
Lindsey Ford
Line Langebek Knudsen
Linnea Brown
Lisa Agostini
Lisa Dillman
Lisa Hess
Lisa Leahigh
Lisa Simpson
Liz Clifford
Liz Starbuck Greer
Lorna Bleach
Lottie Smith
Louise Evans

Louise Greenberg
Louise Jolliffe
Louise Smith
Luc Verstraete
Lucie Taylor
Lucinda Smith
Lucy Huggett
Lucy Moffatt
lucy Scott
Lucy Banks
Luke Healey
Lydia Trethewey
Lynda Graham
Lyndia Thomas
Lynn Fung
Lynn Martin
Madden Aleia
Maeve Lambe
Maggie Kerkman
Maggie Livesey
Marcel Inhoff
Margaret Dillow
Margaret Jull Costa
Margo Gorman
Mari-Liis Calloway
Maria Ahnhem Farrar
Maria Lomunno
Maria Losada
Marie Donnelly
Marie Harper
Marina Castledine
Marion Pennicuik
Marja S Laaksonen
Mark Bridgman
Mark Reynolds
Mark Sargent
Mark Sheets
Mark Sztyber

Mark Waters
Martha W Hood
Martin Brown
Martin Price
Martin Eric Rodgers
Mary Addonizio
Mary Angela Brevidoro
Mary Clarke
Mary Heiss
Mary Wang
Maryse Meijer
Mathieu Trudeau
Matt Carruthers
Matt Davies
Matt Greene
Matt O'Connor
Matthew Adamson
Matthew Banash
Matthew Cooke
Matthew Eatough
Matthew Francis
Matthew Gill
Matthew Lowe
Matthew Woodman
Matthias Rosenberg
Maura Cheeks
Max Cairnduff
Max Longman
Meaghan Delahunt
Meg Lovelock
Megan Wittling
Mel Pryor
Melissa Beck
Melissa da Silveira Serpa
Melissa Quignon-Finch
Melissa Stogsdill

Melissa Wan
Meredith Martin
Michael Aguilar
Michael Bichko
Michael Boog
Michael James
  Eastwood
Michael Floyd
Michael Gavin
Michael Kuhn
Michaela Goff
Michelle Mercaldo
Michelle Perkins
Miguel Head
Mike Turner
Miles Smith-Morris
Moira Weir
Molly Foster
Mona Arshi
Morayma Jimenez
Morgan Lyons
Moriah Haefner
Myles Nolan
N Tsolak
Nancy Jacobson
Nancy Kerkman
Nancy Oakes
Nancy Peters
Nargis McCarthy
Natalia Reyes
Natalie Ricks
Nathalie Teitler
Nathan McNamara
Nathan Rowley
Nathan Weida
Nicholas Brown
Nicholas Rutherford
Nick James

Nick Marshall
Nick Nelson & Rachel
  Eley
Nick Sidwell
Nick Twemlow
Nicola Cook
Nicola Hart
Nicola Sandiford
Nicola Scott
Nicole Matteini
Nigel Fishburn
Niki Sammut
Nina de la Mer
Nina Nickerson
Nina Todorova
Norman Batchelor
Norman Carter
Odilia Corneth
Ohan Hominis
Olivia Powers
Olivia Scott
Olivia Turon
Pamela Ritchie
Pamela Tao
Pankaj Mishra
Pat Winslow
Patrick Hawley
Patrick Hoare
Paul Cray
Paul Ewing
Paul Flaig
Paul Jones
Paul Munday
Paul Myatt
Paul Nightingale
Paul Scott
Paul Segal
Paul Stallard

Paula McGrath
Pavlos Stavropoulos
Penelope Hewett
  Brown
Penelope Hewett-
  Brown
Peter Griffin
Peter Halliday
peter Hayden
Peter McBain
Peter McCambridge
Peter Rowland
Peter Taplin
Peter Watson
Peter Wells
Petra Stapp
Phil Bartlett
Philip Herbert
Philip Warren
Philip Williams
Philipp Jarke
Phillipa Clements
Phoebe McKenzie
Phoebe Millerwhite
Phyllis Reeve
Pia Figge
Piet Van Bockstal
Rachael de Moravia
Rachael Williams
Rachel Adducci
Rachel Gregory
Rachel Matheson
Rachel Van Riel
Rachel Watkins
Ralph Cowling
Ramona Pulsford
Ranbir Sidhu
Rebecca O'Reilly

Rebecca Peer
Rebecca Rosenthal
Rebecca Servadio
Rebecca Shaak
Rebecca Söregi
Rebekka Bremmer
Renee Otmar
Renee Thomas
Rhiannon Armstrong
Rich Sutherland
Richard Clark
Richard Ellis
Richard Gwyn
Richard Mann
Richard Mansell
Richard Priest
Richard Shea
Richard Soundy
Richard Stubbings
Richard White
Riley & Alyssa
  Manning
Rishi Dastidar
Rita Kaar
Rita O'Brien
Robert Gillett
Robert Hannah
Roberto Hull
Robin McLean
Robin Taylor
Roger Newton
Roger Ramsden
Rory Williamson
Rosalind May
Rosalind Ramsay
Rose Crichton
Rosie Ernst Trustram
Ross Beaton

Roxanne O'Del Ablett
Roz Simpson
Rupert Ziziros
Ruth Deyermond
Ryan Day
Ryan Oliver
SK Grout
ST Dabbagh
Sally Baker
Sally Warner
Sam Gordon
Samantha Pavlov
Samantha Walton
Samuel Crosby
Sara Bea
Sara Kittleson
Sara Sherwood
Sara Unwin
Sara Warshawski
Sarah Arboleda
Sarah Brewer
Sarah Duguid
Sarah Lucas
Sarah Pybus
Sarah Spitz
Sasha Dugdale
Scott Astrada
Scott Chiddister
Scott Henkle
Scott Russell
Scott Simpson
Sean Kottke
Sean McDonagh
Sean Myers
Shannon Knapp
Sharon Dogar
Shauna Gilligan
Sheila Packa

Sienna Kang
Simon James
Simon Pitney
Simon Robertson
Simone Martelossi
Stacy Rodgers
Stefanie Schrank
Stefano Mula
Stephan Eggum
Stephanie De Los
  Santos
Stephanie Miller
Stephanie Smee
Stephen Cowley
Stephen Pearsall
Steve Chapman
Steve Clough
Steve Dearden
Steve James
Steve Tuffnell
Steven Norton
Steven Williams
Stewart Eastham
Stu Sherman
Stuart Wilkinson
Su Bonfanti
Sue Davies
Sunny Payson
Susan Jaken
Susan Winter
Suzanne Kirkham
Tallulah Fairfax
Tania Hershman
Tara Roman
Tasmin Maitland
Tatiana Griffin
Teresa Werner
Tess Cohen

Tess Lewis
Tessa Lang
Thom Cuell
Thom Keep
Thomas Alt
Thomas Campbell
Thomas Mitchell
Thomas Smith
Thomas van den
  Bout
Tian Zheng
Tiffany Lehr
Tim Kelly
Tim Nicholls
Tim Scott
Tina Rotherham-
  Winqvist
Toby Halsey

Toby Ryan
Tom Darby
Tom Doyle
Tom Franklin
Tom Gray
Tom Stafford
Tom Whatmore
Tory Jeffay
Tracy Northup
Tracy Shapley
Trent Leleu
Trevor Wald
Turner Docherty
Val & Tom Flechtner
Vanessa Fernandez
  Greene
Vanessa Fuller
Vanessa Heggie

Vanessa Nolan
Victor Meadowcroft
Victoria Goodbody
Vijay Pattisapu
Vikki O'Neill
Wendy Langridge
William Black
William
  Brockenborough
William Franklin
William Mackenzie
William Schwaber
William Sitters
Yoora Yi Tenen
Zachary Maricondia
Zachary Whyte
Zareena Amiruddin
Zoë Brasier

CURRENT & UPCOMING BOOKS